Rebel Wayfarers

MC Saga

Excerpts & Shorts

MariaLisa deMora

Edited by Hot Tree Editing

Collection first Published 2019

Individual copyright dates noted in sections.

ISBN 13: 978-1-946738-55-4

DEDICATION

To the Bibliophiles among us: Those lovers of books; the ones who love to read, admire and collect books.

Contents

ACKNOWLEDGMENTS

Readers make my world go 'round. You are the reason I keep pushing that publish button, and while I still can't believe anyone would want to read my words (Imposter Syndrome is a real deal thing, man) you've proven to me time and again that I'm wrong.

Thank you.

For asking for stories, for loving characters, for being engaged in my worlds in a way that tells me it's "real" for you, too.

Woofully yours,
~ML

Deleted From Mica

#1

MARIALISA DEMORA

J.J.

"J.J., when are the new tractors going to be delivered to our east coast yards? We have drivers sitting on their asses in Wilmington and Savannah who aren't making any money—for themselves or for us. They have families. We have bills. You said the equipment would be there a week ago, but here we still sit, in the same position of—let me say it one more time—not making any money."

Jon Junior, or J.J. to friends and family, waited on the phone without saying anything, knowing from experience that Daniel wasn't done yet. *Wait for it…wait for it…*

"And why is Dickie stuck in Montana waiting for Canadian permits? He missed his appointment with the import agent this morning because of it. We need those permits, man, especially if we're going to take over some of Cochrane's charcoal runs. What the hell have you been doing with your time, J.J.?" And bingo, there it was, the ever-present dig at how long it took him to do anything anymore.

"I dunno, Danny. What do you think I've been doing? Sitting on my ass all day? Well, yeah, I am. Kinda comes with the fucking territory," he said angrily. "Oh, yeah, don't forget—I'm also staying away from the truck bays, trying to stay out of the fucking way of the people doing the real work around here," J.J. shouted into the phone. Smacking the disconnect button several times furiously, he growled, "Goddammit, it's just not as satisfying as smashing a handset down."

A hand came down hard on his shoulder, jarring him out of his anger. "J.J., you need anything, man?" His best friend, Marty Larsen, their chief mechanic, crouched down beside him, putting them at eye level.

"A new fucking life wouldn't hurt, Marty." He took a deep breath and shook his head. "Naw, I'm good, man. It's just Danny being Danny. He's stuck at some hospital in Chicago, so he calls and tries to micromanage shit here."

Marty frowned. "Why's he at the hospital? He sick? You need to go down, or take your mom down, J.J.?"

"Naw, he's there with a friend. He stopped a mugging or some shit, and he's waiting for them to be released. It's nothing to do with him, thank God. That'd be all Mom needed."

J.J. pushed away from his desk, tucking his cell phone into the breast pocket of his jacket. Looking at Marty, he scowled. "Get outta my way, man." He moved his chair towards where his friend was crouching, forcing him to stand and back away. "I gotta check the permit log, find out why Dickie is stuck in the U.S. of A and isn't in Canada, and then find out why he called Danny and not me."

Turning to go out the office door, Marty asked, "You still coming to Hansen's tonight? That little waitress, Penny, has been asking about you."

"Yeah, I'll be there, but only if you get the ten trucks due for maintenance done and back on the line. You need to go and get your guys working, Chief." J.J. waved in dismissal.

Grabbing the wheels of his chair, he rolled over to the file cabinet, frustrated when the files he needed were in the top drawer, but he jacked around until he had what he needed and spread them out over the desktop.

Picking up the phone, he called his brother Richard, who answered with a gruff, "Yeah?"

"Hey, dickhead, which permit is it you think you don't have? I'm showing we applied for everything needed when you were in the shop last week."

Dickie responded, "I was wrong. Everything's good. I'm waiting in line now and should be at the inspection bay in about ten minutes."

J.J. frowned. "Okay, I'll let Danny know. How long did you sit at the border thinking you weren't permitted before you looked and found out you were wrong?"

"Not long, a couple hours maybe," his little brother responded.

"Okay, make sure your logs are in order, man. No more fines, okay?"

Hanging up on his second brother of the morning, J.J. wondered if what he heard in Dickie's voice was a hangover. It wouldn't be the first time, and he strongly suspected that a bottle might've had more to do with missing the appointment in the import agent's inspection bay than Dickie making sure his permits were in order. His brother usually depended on the mechanics to do that for him, along with pretty much everything else except actually driving the rig.

At the end of the day, Marty came dragging back into J.J.'s office, flopping down in the chair with a sigh, asking, "Hansen's?"

J.J. nodded at him, no less exhausted. "Lemme lock up and grab my truck. I'll meet you there."

"Truck keys," Marty demanded, holding out his hand, and he waited until J.J. tossed them over, "I'll start it for ya."

At his truck, after locking up, J.J. attached the winch to the hook on his chair and leveraged himself into the driver seat. Using the controls to place the chair in the back, he closed the door and waited in the warm truck until Marty drove out the gate ahead of him. Pulling up at Hansen's, the local bar, he reversed the process and met Marty inside at their normal table.

"Penny's working tonight, man." Marty nudged his shoulder. "And she's comin' this way." J.J. rolled his eyes, looking at the eagerness in his friend's face, but not wanting to put a damper on his enjoyment.

"Hey, J.J., Marty, how was work today?" She sat their usual beers down—two bottles of Booyah, a local favorite.

Marty responded, “Same old, same old, Penny.”

Looking around the bar, J.J. said, “Y’all are pretty busy tonight. Working by yourself?”

“Nancy should be in anytime now. I’m off at ten,” she tossed over her shoulder at the two men as she walked back to the bar.

J.J. restricted himself to a single beer, as he’d done for the last year. There was avid conversation between Marty and his friends about the Mallets’ chances this year; Daniel’s team was always a hot topic during hockey season.

After a few hours, he was ready to go home. There was no sense hanging around a bar if you weren’t drinking; plus, he was tired and getting hungry. Telling the guys goodnight and leaving Hansen’s, he saw Penny standing outside by her car, which had the hood up. “What’s up?” He rolled towards her.

“My stinkin’ battery’s dead. I hate winter.” She kicked her car tire.

“Gimme a minute. I have jumpers.” He moved to go back towards his truck, pushing hard through the slushy snow just as a group of men came out of the bar. One of them saw Penny, and assuming what had happened, grabbed cables from his own backseat before J.J. could even get to the toolbox on his truck. He sighed and waved goodbye at Penny, knowing she’d be gone before he could make it back across the parking lot. Twisting in his chair, he started the process of getting into his truck to go home.

Finally at home, J.J. could relax, wheeling slowly into his bedroom. Danny had remodeled the entire house for him after the accident, and everything was set up for easy wheelchair access. Grabbing an overhead bar, he shifted to the bench near the open shelving that served as his clothing storage. Stripping bare, he put a towel down across the seat of the chair and moved back, heading in for a hot shower. Sitting in the steam, J.J.'s thoughts turned back to more than a year ago—the day everything went to shit, when he was sentenced to this chair and this life.

He'd been standing to the side of one of the tractors, reading a clipboard of the maintenance needed for this rig. He was watching idly as Dickie ran the lift to pick up the tractor so the mechanic could work on it. There was an abrupt grinding noise and then shouting. Something picked J.J. up and threw him face first into the wall, trapping him there. He had pushed ineffectually at the wall, unable to move away.

Twisting and seeing what had him pinned, he knew why he couldn't move. The tractor had slipped off the lift, and he was immobilized between the big wheels of the rear axle and the bay wall. He was surprised there was no pain, and he could clearly hear everyone yelling at once, but there were no constructive suggestions.

It figured he'd have to organize his own rescue. "Hey, Marty," he yelled, "call 911," and people quieted down some. "Dickie, see if you can get the lift back down. Maybe the truck will slide back. I'm stuck, man. I can't move here."

He heard Marty yelling into the phone, and twisted the other way to see Dickie looking at him with horror on his face. "Richard Rupert, see if you can put the lift back down," he barked out an order as if he was still in the army, using his brother's proper name to try to snap him out of it, and as he did so, he felt a twinge of something not-quite-painful in his lower back. Dickie didn't shift, just kept looking at him.

"Don't move, J.J. Don't move anything," Marty screamed at them. "The ambulance is on the way." Sliding as best he could between the truck and the wall in order to be next to J.J., he started asking questions. "Where do you hurt? Can you breathe okay? Where are you bleeding?"

J.J. shook his head. "I'm just pinned, Marty. Get the damned truck off me."

Shaking his own head, Marty said, "Not moving you until the ambulance folks get here, J.J. Just stay with me, man." Marty's voice was high with tension and fear, and J.J. wondered what he could see from where he was standing.

J.J. felt something wet on his chin and lifted a hand to wipe the spit away, but his hand came away red. That should mean something, but he couldn't decide what, because he was getting tired. "Marty, I'm tired, man. Call Danny...tell him I'm going home?"

Marty's eyes were big in his face. "Sure, sure, J.J., I'll call Danny. Stay with me..."

And J.J. didn't hear anything else for a while.

Waking days later in the hospital, J.J. found he no longer had a spleen, one of his kidneys, an appendix, or a gallbladder. Apparently, the docs had cleaned house while they were inside him, taking out all his spare parts. He had also lost the ability to walk. He could feel nothing below his pelvis, and his legs were like dead wood. He was paralyzed.

Pulling himself from the memories, J.J. shook his head free of the water droplets and turned off the shower. He grabbed a towel off the warming rack, drying his skin roughly, rubbing viciously at the scars on his belly. Then, he began with what he thought of as his suck-it-up routine. He knew he was lucky. He had his life, and his family, and a job he still loved most days. He had few things to complain about, other than the accident. Dragging a shirt and shorts onto his frame, he headed to the kitchen to make dinner, wondering if his brother was still stuck in the hospital in Chicago.

A SWEET & MERRY CHRISTMAS

#1.5

MARIALISA DEMORA

DEDICATION

To all the Jessicas and Brandys I know and love. I hope you find your happy, in whatever flavor that happens to be.

A SWEET & MERRY CHRISTMAS

Rub a dub, dub, two girls in a … biker bar? We've got bikers and bakers and bartenders, but will they embrace more than the Christmas spirit?

A sweet Christmas short story of want and desire. Experience a taste of Brandy's pursuit of Jess, and their coming together for the first time. You might even get to catch a glimpse of many of your favorite Rebels at this holiday celebration, in true Mason style.

This short story gives a little insight into a sweet couple who many readers have asked about. In the series timeline, this story would sit alongside book #1, Mica.

ACKNOWLEDGMENTS

Thank you to the readers who kept asking about Jess and Brandy, wanting to know more about the dynamics of their relationship and how they met. See what happens when you tell me you want something? Muuuwah, love alla you guys.

Woofully yours,
~ML

A Sweet & Merry Christmas

This story falls right in line with Mica, and actually predates that series beginner by a short period. But, it can be
read at any time without spoilers.

Brandy

"You're just in time! Pull up a stool, help me ice these last ones," Brandy Still called across the bakery, lifting her head to smile at the petite woman who'd just walked in the door from the outside. The bundled-up form raised a hand with a noncommittal grunt, and began the process of divesting herself of the seasonal wear necessary to survive a Chicago winter.

Gloves first, revealing slim, white fingers, then the scarf was carefully unwrapped from a slender column of throat, and Brandy caught her breath. She loved watching Jessica Nalan do nearly anything, but seeing her undressing, even if it was just the outer layer of clothing she wore, made desire clench deep in her belly.

Next was the patchwork toque, tugged roughly off leaving the short, pixie cut standing on end, her small fingers threading through her blonde hair and bringing it back to some semblance of order. Brandy stood, still watching as those same fingers deftly maneuvered the zipper of the coat down past breasts and belly, the edges of the coat falling open to be shoved aside when Jess removed the garment entirely, draping it over a nearby chair.

"Let me wash my hands. I'll be right back to help," Jess said, and Brandy tilted her head questioningly. "You told me to help you ice cupcakes, dork. Did you forget already?"

Laughing, Brandy turned back to the tray of individual cakes on the counter. "Yeah, right. I guess I just didn't think you'd take me serious." *Shit*, she thought, *I need to watch myself. I can't get lost watching her like that, or she's going to figure things out.*

Piping buttercream icing on top of the cupcakes, she was creating small cream-colored Christmas trees, wreaths, reindeer, and candy canes, one after the other. She hadn't heard the swinging door that lead to the rear of the shop, but Jess had probably headed back already. If she wasn't just putting her coat back on after seeing Brandy drooling over her.

She let out a surprised "Eeep" when she felt cold hands push under her shirt and place themselves palm-first against the small of her back. Twisting away, she scolded Jess, "Your hands are cold!"

"And you are warm," she heard, but suddenly couldn't concentrate on the words or the voice because those hands had slipped to her sides, cupping around her ribs and tugging her backwards slightly, holding her in place. Her breath caught in her throat, if Jess knew what this did to her, she'd move away, take the warmth of her hands from her skin, the heat of her body from Brandy's back.

She'd first noticed Jess on the campus of the college they both attended, but the woman had stuck close to her roommate, Mica Scott, and Brandy had never been certain if they were a couple or not. It wasn't until they'd graduated and all moved to Chicago that they'd become friends, and she decided Mica wasn't Jess' lover, glad she'd kept her questions to herself. She was sure Jess still didn't know her sexual preferences, and Brandy was happy to keep a lid on it in order to stay friends with her.

She'd seen firsthand the cruel wedge that could be driven into a friendship when she admitted being interested in women...even when she hadn't been attracted to that friend. She could just imagine the Grand Canyon-sized gulf that would be created if she confessed her desires to Jess, who she'd lusted after for a long time. So, she would just continue to hunger from a distance, trying to hide her longing.

But those hands...those damn hands were still curled around her sides, slipping down to her waist and then back up, it nearly felt like a caress. Brandy closed her eyes, concentrating on the feel of Jess' now-warm hands on her, fingers pressing into her skin, trailing up and down her ribs, the tie of her apron no deterrent to the touch. Soft, fingertips questing along the top of her jeans, tracing the edge of the waistband around to the snap closure.

The small woman was a furnace behind her; Brandy could feel her breasts pressed against her back. Hardly daring to breathe, she felt a kiss on her spine at the same time those fingertips tugged at the snap, loosening it before delving underneath. "Jess," she whispered, not sure what else to say, desperate to not derail this moment she'd wanted for so long.

One hand drifted up her side, and she felt the barest brush of fingertips across the side of her breast, a slight graze across her nipple which pebbled and hardened under the attention. Gently tracing along the upper curve of her mound, Jess hooked one finger under the lace, tugging the fabric down, allowing her breast to spill over the top of the cup and into her warm palm. Exposed to her bare touch, Brandy felt a drawing sensation in her breast, the tug reaching down from her hard nipple through her body to her clit, throbbing in time with her fast-beating heart.

Another kiss on her spine and the woman's second hand flattened against her belly before sliding downward into her pants. Slipping into the front of her panties, Jess' fingers pressed into her, and she heard a small gasp behind her when they first touched her slippery wetness, evidence of her arousal. She felt the delicate rasp of a fingernail dragged across her clit once...twice, before the hand pushed further, pressing what felt like two fingers deep inside her.

Involuntarily her hips thrust forward, her back arching, shoulders pressing back against the woman plastered against her. Wordlessly Jess worked her, tugging and pinching on her nipple in a rhythm sympathetic to the movements against and inside her pussy, bringing her closer...drawing her upward, relentlessly dragging her into the deep waves before pushing her over the top, holding her tightly as she quivered in her arms.

Dropping her head forward, she looked down to see...the expanse of her icing-dotted apron, fabric moving slightly with her gasping breaths. She felt suddenly bereft, thinking, *I won't even have the memory of what her fingers looked like against my skin.* One of her hands was still holding the sleeve of icing and she saw the thick mixture pressing against the tip of the bag as her hand tightened around it, her other hand gripping the edge of the cabinet tightly.

Maybe she doesn't know what to say, she thought, even as she felt Jess' fingers righting her clothing, pulling the cup of her bra back over the nipple and breast, the other hand tugging her zipper up and fastening the snap on her jeans.

Say something, she heard the quiet plea and realized Jess must be even more frightened than she was. *Brandy, please...*

Taking a deep breath, she laid down the pastry bag and turned, not caring that she had sugar coating her hands she began to reach out and then halted abruptly, seeing Jess still across the room, just now laying her coat across the back of the chair. Closing her eyes in despair, she realized she'd imagined the entire encounter. Nothing had happened...nothing could happen.

Swallowing hard, she forced a smile onto her face, "Slowpoke, get a move on it. Wash those nasty" *delicious* "fingers and get back out here" *back inside me* "and help me finish this order for Mason."

Jess grinned, "Since when does Mason order cupcakes?" Mason was the president of a Chicago-based motorcycle club that Mica had moved in next to earlier this year. He'd developed a fondness for Mica, and Brandy had grown to like and respect the man when she saw how gently he treated both of her friends, behaving as if Jess and Mica were more like little sisters than attractive, unattached young women.

"Since he's having a party at Jackson's, I guess," Brandy turned back to the counter and took a deep breath. She'd had fantasies about Jess before but never like that, at work and standing upright…and never with the woman in the room. Calling loudly, she asked, "Bring one of the trays with you when you come back?"

"You got it," she heard a yell from the back room, and then the door swung outward, and Jess came through, balancing two trays. "Two is better than one, right?" she asked, laughing.

"Yeah, thanks." She reached up to grab the box of edible decorations, sliding it across the countertop to Jess. "Sprinkles are in here, lots of colors. There are some other things like cinnamon bits for reindeer noses, candy for ornaments. Go crazy, woman. Make the cupcakes beautiful."

Jess grinned up at her; a smile lifting the corners of her eyes and turning the lovely woman into a spectacularly beautiful one and Brandy watched mesmerized as Jess licked across her bottom lip. "Am I allowed to taste-test?"

God, yes. Please. "You bet, go for it. Just don't make yourself sick. Folks are bringing sandwiches and snacks to the party, so there will be real food there tonight in addition to the cakes we're taking." Brandy massaged the pastry bag of icing briefly, trying unsuccessfully to not think about doing the same to Jess' ass, and then got started icing the rest of the cupcakes.

They worked side-by-side for a couple hours, mostly in companionable silence, only broken by brief questions about the flavors, or when they paused to laugh at a cupcake Jess destroyed. That had been another moment when Brandy's breath caught in her throat, because Jess broke the cake apart, and fed one half to Brandy piece by piece, her gamine features grinning up at Brandy the entire time, her fingers occasionally trailing across Brandy's lips in an unconscious tease.

When the chore was done, Brandy leaned back against the counter, looking at the stacks of boxes filled with iced and decorated cupcakes, ready to be packed in her car for the trip across town to Jackson's, the bar Mason owned. Brandy groaned inwardly when she looked at Jess, who was studiously licking her fingers clean of icing. The woman was going to kill her. She mused, *Is it possible to die from desire*?

Loading up the sweet treats, she casually suggested Jess ride with her, and before she knew it, they were locked in her van barreling up the road with Jess controlling the music. Laughing as they pulled into the parking lot at the bar, they were both singing to silly, seasonal tunes and she glanced over as she parked, catching a look she couldn't quite define on Jess' face. Their gaze locked for a second, then Brandy forced hers away, bending her head to avoid looking at Jess again while they gathered up their gloves and scarves, preparing to exit the vehicle.

At the back of the van, she was still struggling with her gloves when she heard Jess say from right beside her, "Hold still." Freezing in place, she felt fingers dipping alongside her neck, under her scarf, then tugging it up and over her mouth and nose, the cloth of gloves grazing her skin as the fingers retreated. Forcing her lungs to work again, she muttered, "Thanks," and opened the doors of the van.

Before she could lift out the first stack of boxes, she heard movement from behind them and swung to see a group of men walking their way. She stilled because she didn't recognize any of them, and the man in the lead barked out a humorless laugh. "Do you know where you are, pretty lady? Lady as good-looking as you should be more careful where you show up." The men walking with him laughed mockingly, spreading out to the sides, sweeping towards her and Jess like the outstretched wings of a bird, herding them back towards the open van.

One of the men had gotten close enough to reach out a hand, tugging Jess' toque off her head and tossing it to the side. Brandy moved without thinking, putting herself between the small woman and the large, intimidating man. "Don't touch her," she hissed between tightly clenched teeth, leaning towards him as she shoved Jess backward, away from the man.

One of the other men made a crude comment, and she felt a tugging at her arm. Reaching back her hand, she felt small fingers thread between hers and she squeezed reassuringly. Speaking to the leader, she said, "We're here by invitation, asshole. And yes, I know where I am."

There was a shout from across the parking lot and the men in front of her and Jess parted like batter before a knife, revealing a set of faces she did know, and was damned glad to see right now. "Slate," she called, squeezing Jess' hand again, not letting go.

"Brandy," he responded with a scowl on his handsome face, she could see his forehead wrinkling from a dozen paces away and she relaxed a tiny bit. *He'll take care of us*, she thought. "Fucktards, what the hell do you think you are doing?" That was directed to the men now edging further away from her van.

"Slate, man. We didn't know they were Rebel pussy. Respect, man." The leader spoke the words, but his leer left no doubt that he'd have rather not been interrupted.

"I believe the term you are looking for is a friend of the Rebel club, dildo." That was from one of the men with Slate, a man named Roach that she knew Mica was fond of.

"No shit?" the man said, rocking back on his heels. "Two pussies as Rebel 'friends'? Well ain't that just an interesting state of affairs." He sneered at Roach and looked up at another of the Rebels. "Tugboat, does Mason know you got little 'friends' like this?"

"What the fuck is your problem, dickhead?" The statement came from Tug, an older man with striking features, his white hair swept back from his head with a bandanna, dark mustache framing a mouth now drawn down in displeasure. "Dominos want a shitstorm? You're fucking standing on Rebel ground. I'm telling you one time, you want a shitstorm then you keep going the way you're going, man and you will fucking get it." He asked again, "What is your fucking problem?"

"No problem, Tugboat. We were just making sure the ladies were certain of their welcome. No disrespect, man." That was the man who'd thrown Jess' hat on the ground, he bent over now and retrieved it, holding it out towards her. Brandy intercepted, grabbing it from his hand, angered to see him touching any part of Jess, even something as innocent as her hat. She ground her teeth and her hand tightened around it, crushing it in her fist.

"Then if there's no problem, you won't mind moving on," Slate said, folding his arms across his chest, stepping between the women and the men. Without looking away from the leader, he addressed Tug, "You got this, brother?"

"Fuck yeah, I got this," was the response and Slate turned his back on the two groups, moving to face Brandy and Jess. His voice softened when he spoke to them, "Y'all bring dessert, Brandy?" He sniffed and made a show of rolling his eyes. "*Goddamn* that van smells good. How the hell both of you are so fucking tiny is beyond me. If I had to work around this good smellin' shit all day, I'd weigh a ton."

Brandy laughed, "And you'd still be good lookin'."

He reached out and cupped a hand behind Brandy's neck, pulling her close for a hug. "Brown Sugar Brandy, you okay, babe?" he whispered into her ear and she nodded, saying softly, "Yeah."

He stepped back and looked down at their hands, smiling at their fingers still twined together. "Jess, you okay, honey?"

Brandy turned around in time to see a bright blush working its way up Jess' face, coloring her cheeks and then the tips of her ears. "Yeah," she said. "I'm okay." She pulled at

Brandy's hand and without letting go, brought Brandy toward her. "Can I have my hat back, Brand?"

She brought the toque up and pressed it into the hand she was still holding, then freed Jess, smiling privately when the hold appeared reluctantly released. "Here you go." Turning to look behind Slate, she realized the other group of men had disappeared and the Rebels were already walking back towards them. "I have quite a few boxes to take inside for the party. Do you think you guys could help out?"

Slate nodded and whistled, drawing the attention of the Rebels. "Tote and carry, boys. Let's get these ladies inside and out of the cold." He nodded an apparent question at Tug who was wiping his hand with a bandana, and received a brusque nod in return. Smiling grimly, he moved to reach into the van, pulling out the first stack of boxes. "We got this, Brandy. Why don't you and Jess go on inside? Merry is already in there getting everything set up." Merry was a long-time waitress and bartender at Jackson's, and a friend to both of the women.

Inside the bar, everyone pitched in, setting up tables and generally getting ready for a big, informal party. The irony of the set-up wasn't lost on Brandy and she snorted a laugh that Jess heard, causing her to tilt her head and ask, "What?"

"If you'd told me two years ago that I'd be excitedly waiting to exchange secret Santa gifts with a bunch of bikers, I'd have checked you for a head injury." She laughed, shaking her head. "This is pretty remarkable, though. It's cool that Mason organized all of this, that he'd put together a party for the Rebels and us. I've never felt safer than when we're hanging out with them, and they are all sweet, amazing guys."

"Glad to hear you think so, babe," she heard a deep voice say from behind her and watched as Jess ran around her, squealing with happiness.

She turned to see Mason with his arms wrapped around Jess' shoulders, his cheek laid on top of her head while he smiled at Brandy. Holding out his other hand, he reached and grabbed her by the wrist, pulling her into an embrace, slipping his arm around her shoulders, too. "Hey Mason," she said fondly. "I brought both the truffles and custard-filled cupcakes for you. Just you, mind," she scolded, looking over where Slate was standing, a cupcake already in his hand. He shrugged, shoving the cake into his mouth and holding out his hands in a 'who me' motion, and they all laughed.

A couple hours later she was sitting on a stool at the bar, resting her elbows on the edge. Merry had set a perfectly dirty martini in front of her a few minutes ago and she sipped it gratefully. Looking down the bar, she saw Jess in deep conversation with Tug and smiled. Those two were the biggest jokers in the room, and seeing them having a serious discussion was a mystery. She heard the stool on her other side pulled back, and turned to see Slate seating himself. Nodding at him, she picked up her glass and looked back at Jess, freezing when both she and Tug were staring at her.

Quickly turning back to Slate, she caught a look of amusement on his face and he shook his head at her. Picking up his beer, he paused with the edge of the bottle at his lips and asked, "Why don't you just tell her how you feel, sweetheart?"

Brandy looked down at the bar top and shook her head. "She's not the girl for me, unfortunately." She looked up, using the mirror to watch Jess, smiling softly at the play of emotions across the woman's face.

"You can't know that if you haven't made your play, woman." He caught her eyes in the mirror. "You could talk to her tonight, I set the bedroom in the back aside for you when you started drinking, so you ain't going anywhere any time soon, sweetheart. Tug's got your keys and he's under orders to keep you safe, which means you don't leave until he says so. You could invite her to the back...just sayin'."

"I don't want to lose her friendship." She shook her head. "It's not worth the risk."

He held out his left arm, pushing his shirt sleeve up to his elbow and smoothed his skin with his hand, drawing her attention to the tattoo there. "Never let your fear decide your fate," he said, reading the words inked on his skin next to a beautifully detailed compass. "What if you're wrong, sweetheart? What if you could have both?" he asked, looking past her, then back at her face. Smiling, he stood from the stool and in a sing-song voice said, "I know something you don't know."

"What?" she asked and then balled up her napkin, throwing it at him as he walked away without answering her question. "Asshole," she called after him and heard a snort of laughter behind her.

Turning she saw Mason had walked up and was standing between her and Tug. He didn't look at her directly, like Slate had, he caught her gaze in the mirror. "Thanks for this, babe. It's been a good night."

"Yeah, it's been fun to watch everyone open their gifts, and have a good time." She fingered her new earrings. "Who knew Red had such good taste in jewelry." She tilted her head, looking at him. "Did you like your boots? I have the receipt, if you want to return them."

He shook his head, reaching out to pat the back of her hand lying on the bar top. "They fit perfectly, babe. Thank you. Boots are a pain in the ass to buy, mostly because I just fucking hate shopping. I couldn't have asked for a better gift." She smiled, and they both turned to look across the bar when shouts of laughter erupted near the pool tables.

"Looks like Mica's cleaning up again. Poor Digger, he won't have any money left after tonight." She smiled, peeking over his shoulder to see if she could catch a glimpse of Jess, but Tug was standing alone now. Sighing, she leaned on the bar and picked up her glass. Taking a drink, she met Mason's gaze in the mirror again. "It's been a good party, Mason."

He nodded, pushing away from the bar. "Yeah, brothers and friends are important. It's good to remember that, keep 'em close, and Christmas gives us a good excuse."

She watched him stalk over towards where Mica was schooling one of the Rebels in the fine art of eight-ball. The tall biker was standing close to Mica, but with a glance to his president, Digger stepped away, nervously twisting the stick in his hands.

Mason stopped short of where they were playing and he leaned against the wall, his eyes hungrily following every move Mica made, his body language loud and clear. Brandy shook her head, the man had it bad for her. None of the

Rebels she'd talked to knew why he didn't just make a move, because they were all relatively sure Mica'd be open to an offer from the authoritative biker.

He was influential and powerful, and Brandy thought he'd probably be dominant in bed. But, she mused, maybe that was what kept Mica separate from him, her history might not lend itself to exploring that side of things again...not just now, but maybe ever.

Holding her hand over the top of her glass when Merry would have refilled it, she turned on the stool, leaning both elbows on the wooden edge, surveying the room. There were little groups of men scattered throughout the bar, without exception they all wore leather or denim vests with a variety of patches sewn to the material. Most had the name of the motorcycle club at the top of their back, and the emblem that represented the club just below that. Some of the men had town names across the bottom of their vests, and some had other words like 'Prospect', 'Gypsy', or 'National' that designated their position in the club.

She saw Tug was now seated in a booth by himself and climbed off the stool, walking over and sitting beside him. He scooted over to give her room, sliding his arm across the back of the bench and curved it around her shoulders. He hugged her tightly for a minute, loudly kissing the side of her head, then he sat back and looked down at her. "Having a good time, pretty lady?"

"I am," she said with a smile. "What did you get from your Santa?" She patted his thigh and leaned into his side, relaxing in the safety of his embrace.

"Got a new wallet. It's pretty cool, lookit." He shifted, pulling the wallet from his back pocket, twisting the chain that attached to his belt loop out of the way, showing her the tooling on the leather.

Smiling she nodded, "Who was your Santa?"

"Tats," he laughed. "The man did good, but he got shortchanged, his Santa got him fringed gloves. Can you see that man wearing fringed riding gloves?"

"Oh no," she said with a grin. "Who was his Santa?"

Tug laughed harder, "Me."

Throwing her head back and laughing hard, she told him, "You are an evil, evil man." He nodded in agreement and picked up his beer, taking a drink.

She felt a pressure on her side and turned to look, seeing Jess squeezing onto the bench beside her. "Scooch over, woman," Jess said, pushing on her hip with her own. Tug shifted, and Brandy moved with him, making room for Jess at the end of the seat.

Tug complained, "There was a whole other seat over there, girl. You didn't have to work so hard at squishing me."

Wrapping her hand around Brandy's wrist, she pulled her hand over, threading their fingers together. "Yeah, but then I couldn't sit next to my hero."

Tug nodded, "She was damned fierce in the lot, wasn't she? Ready to take that fucktard on all by herself."

"She was," Jess agreed, her hand helping warm Brandy's suddenly-freezing fingers. "She got right up in that dude's face. Called him out for picking on little, old me."

Brandy turned her head back and forth, following the conversation with a grin on her face.

"Not the smartest thing she could have done," he said, leaning forward to look across Brandy at Jess. "But fierce. Protecting her own. Gotta respect that, right?"

"Yeah, she was protecting me," Jess said, a note of surprise in her voice that made Brandy wonder how much she'd had to drink so far tonight. "Does that mean—Tug, does that mean I could be hers?"

God, I wish, she thought, licking her lips.

"Might do so, little one," he said softly, turning to look into Brandy's face. "Might mean just that, honey."

Jess leaned into her side, and Brandy shivered at the contact, her breath rapid and shallow and she bit her lips, closing her eyes. She felt an absence on her other side, and opened her eyes to find Tug extricating himself from the booth, climbing over the back of the high-backed bench. He smiled at her and nodded as he swung his legs over, leaving her and Jess sitting alone in the booth.

Resting her head on Brandy's shoulder, Jess wiggled in the seat, making herself more comfortable and opening her mouth in a wide yawn. "I'm getting tired," she complained, "Mica had us in the office early today, getting a presentation ready for some douche that didn't even show for his meeting." She yawned again, and Brandy made a sympathetic noise. She didn't think she could speak coherently right now if she'd tried.

"Tug said we're staying here tonight," Jess rubbed her cheek up and down on Brandy's collarbone, lightly smacking her lips before yawning again.

Nodding in agreement, Brandy was acutely aware of every inch of Jess' body that was touching hers. From the soft skin between her fingers, the pad of her thumb tracing slowly back and forth across the sensitive inside of Brandy's wrist, to her strong arm draped across Brandy's thigh. Jess' hip, pressed against hers where she rested on the seat, the heat from her body where her side lay along Brandy's ribs. Jess' head softly resting on her shoulder, her hair tickling the bare skin of her neck and jaw.

"Do you know which room Tug meant?" Jess asked quietly.

"Yeah," she whispered. "Want me to show you?"

Slowly peeling herself from Brandy's side, Jess stood but kept their hands twined together. Nodding, she said, "Yeah, I'd like that a lot."

Brandy looked up at her, wondering if Jess knew what she was implying, and then the woman smiled at her and she knew...knew that this feeling was happening on both sides, that Jess wanted her, too. Standing, she looked down at Jess, raising her unencumbered hand to cup the face she'd wanted to touch for so long, leaning in to dust her lips gently across Jess'. Pulling back to gauge the reaction, she was gratified to see Jess' eyes closed, lashes resting on her cheeks, lips parted in a smile.

Walking towards the door set in the wall behind the bar, Brandy became aware of a stillness in the bar, and she turned to see many of the men were watching them. Slate raised two fingers to his brow, saluting her with a grin before he turned back to the group of men he was standing with. After his acknowledgment of their departure, the noise level gradually rose to normal levels again. Then they were through the door, and Jess was closing it softly behind them, shutting out the sounds from the party.

Is this really happening? she thought, remembering her lapse in the shop that afternoon. Then she felt Jess' hand cupping around her arm, sliding up and down slowly, sensuously touching her and affecting her equilibrium. "Brandy?" she heard the question in Jess' voice and answered her softly.

"Yeah?" *I'm so off balance,* she thought. *I just want to love her.*

"You want this, right?" The hesitation and uncertainty in Jess' tone nearly broke her heart, and she quickly turned, dropping Jess' hand to cup her palms to both of the woman's cheeks.

"Oh, yeah, I do. More than you know." The last syllables were spoken on an outrush of breath against Jess' lips, then she brushed her mouth across softly, gently. Keeping the kiss slow, exploring the taste and feel she'd longed for, she paused to drag her nose up Jess' then back down, and then hungrily captured that addictive mouth with hers again. She smiled when the lips parted effortlessly underneath the gentle pressure, and taking advantage of the opening, she dipped her tongue inside, twisting and twirling with Jess'. She groaned at hearing now desperate gasps for breath that came from the woman she wanted for her lover.

Stepping back, she reached down, clasping Jess' hand again and drew her up the hallway to the first door on the left. "Bedroom," she said, hearing the catch in her own voice.

Leaving the light off, she closed and locked the door behind them, pulling Jess towards the bed sitting in the middle of the room. Tugging her shirt off, she tossed it onto the chair along the wall and reached out to grasp the hem of Jess' shirt, pulling it up and off.

Stepping closer, she pressed her body against Jess, gasping as the woman's hands wrapped around her, unfamiliar but so familiar fingers unfastening her bra so that it fell loosely down her arms. Dropping it to the floor, she slowly and carefully removed Jess' bra, trailing her fingers and thumbs across the now-exposed breasts, pulling and tugging on already erect nipples. Moving closer again, she kissed Jess, their naked torsos rubbing and pressing against the other.

In the low light cast underneath the door from the hallway, Brandy could barely see Jess' face, but could still read the lust written there, and she sighed. "Jess, baby," she said, feeling the sudden motionlessness as Jess stilled underneath her hands. "I don't want to lose your friendship."

Clearing her throat, Jess said hesitantly, "Okay."

The single word didn't give Brandy enough to go on, and she repeated herself. "I can't lose you as a friend, you mean too much to me."

Jess turned her head to the side, and Brandy could only see portions of her face, the angle of her cheekbone, the downturned edge of her mouth. Lifting her hand, she trailed her thumb across Jess' lips, leaning in to kiss her softly. "I want this, so much. *God I want it*. But I want to be able to keep you in my life more."

"So you think this is a one-time thing?" The words and tone were harsh, and Brandy dragged in a painful breath. Jess continued, "Brandy if this is the alcohol talking; then we can just share a bed like we've done in the past. Nothing has to happen, baby. Not if you don't want it."

Shaking her head, Brandy rushed to reassure her, the words stumbling off her tongue. "No, no. I want this. I've wanted you for so long...wanted this. I just don't want to ruin what we already have." She wrapped her arms around Jess, pulling their bodies close, palms slipping up and down her back.

Jess lifted her head, looking at Brandy steadily. "You already have me."

Burying her head in Jess' neck, she took a couple of unsteady breaths, senses stolen by those four words.

Unfastening the closure on Jess' pants, Brandy pushed them down her thighs, taking her panties with them. They both laughed when her legs were shackled by the jeans because they'd forgotten the existence of her winter boots, and Brandy knelt on the floor beside the bed, slipping them off.

Moving to sit on the edge of the bed next to Jess, she watched as the pants were discarded, then her own hands slowed as Jess crawled up into the bed, wagging her naked ass back and forth temptingly. Shaking her head in amusement, Brandy rushed to disrobe and slid up into the bed beside Jess, shivering as their skin met and brushed against each other all along their bodies.

Brandy trailed her fingertips up Jess' stomach, looking down to see the stark contrast between her dark and Jess' light skin, rapt at the sight as her hand slid up and up, the edge of her palm grazing a soft breast, fingers spreading wide to cup and caress. Jess moaned softly and Brandy moved to capture her mouth again, eating down the sounds Jess made as she touched her, discovering all the places that made her lover crazy with desire, the things that set her twisting underneath Brandy's hands and mouth.

She slipped her leg between Jess', pressing hard against the apex of her thighs, encouraging Jess to thrust and rub as she wanted...needed. Brandy kept her hands and mouth busy stroking Jess' breasts and neck, trailing kisses up her jaw to bite at her lips until she was breathless and crying out from the teasing touches and the friction against her clit.

Sliding down Jess' body, she moved between her legs, kissing down her chest and soft belly. Drawing a laugh when she dipped her tongue into Jess' bellybutton, she nipped and bit from hip to hip, her hands pressing those pale thighs apart. She shifted Jess' legs, propping her heels on her shoulders, pushing them wide, so she was open to her.

Running her hands along Jess' inner thighs, she trailed her fingertips from the back of her knees up to where her legs joined her body, following every touch with a slow lick and a soft, sucking kiss. Using her thumbs, she spread the bared pussy and darted her tongue just inside the entrance, lapping and nibbling, working her way up and down, taking her time to bring Jess to the edge of orgasm several times. Brandy's fingers plunged deep, dragging the sweet wetness she found there up to where her mouth waited, sucking, and nibbling on Jess' clit.

Feeling Jess' hands smoothing across her forehead and cheeks, she lifted her gaze, looking up along Jess' body to see her face, eyes wide and unfocused, mouth open with groaning, panting breaths and Brandy smiled. Dropping her face back to Jess' pussy, she buried her mouth, using her lips, tongue, teeth, and fingers to urge Jess to that place of stillness just before the explosion. That instant where the chasing...the frantic seeking is over, and all that's left is to ride the roller coaster down.

Feeling that moment when things began to crash in on Jess, she thrust her fingers in deep, curling and twisting them inside her lover, her tongue stroking rapidly across the perceptibly thrumming clit under her mouth. She heard Jess' voice calling her name, the sound hanging on the air and without thought she pushed one hand down underneath her own body, fingers finding her clit. Tugging and pulling, hips pumping and thrusting against the mattress, she came hard, hand trapped between her heat and the softness of the bed, lips and other hand still working Jess' pussy, drawing out both their climaxes as far as possible.

Resting her cheek against Jess' thigh in the aftermath, she licked her lips as she watched the tension leave her lover's features. In the low light she saw as Jess slowly gained the loose, relaxed look of a well-loved woman, and Brandy smiled again. *I love how she looks right now, in this moment*, she thought. Moving up in the bed to lie beside Jess, she pulled the woman into her side, arranging her head and rolling to press her lips against Jess' forehead.

"That was amazing," she whispered, her eyelids dipping and slipping closed. Sighing, she murmured, "Merry Christmas, Jess." Distantly she was aware of Jess shifting to pull the covers up and over them both, then settling back into her place at Brandy's side, she felt the soft kisses Jess placed across her shoulder and up her neck.

"Yeah, it was," Jess whispered back. "Merry Christmas, babe."

***

In the hallway outside, Mason straightened from where he'd paused, leaning against the wall, a soft smile on his face. If the sounds that he'd overheard from inside the bedroom were any indication, the two women he'd watched dancing around each other for months had finally come together with spectacular results.

Through the open door, he saw Mica still circulating through the men in the bar, and he sighed. Watching as she looked around the room, then smiled brightly when she spotted him, lifting her hand in a quick wave, he thought to himself, *Merry Fucking Christmas to all of us.*

***

From me to you, Merry Christmas!

~ML (2014)

MASON'S MUSINGS

MARIALISA DEMORA

Facebook Group
Blog entry

So Fuckin' Blessed

This blog post by Mason fits into the RWMC following Mason, book #6.

Mason

Mornin'. I hope you're havin' a fine start to your day.

I've been blessed, and I well know it.

Love of a good woman.

Healthy kids.

Strong brotherhood.

Yesterday, however, was a special day.

See, PBJ's got this barn thing where he keeps his dogs. Gots a bunch of land, too, so we use it when we wanna have fun gettin' dirty, or have a rowdier bonfire than we can at the in-town clubhouse.

I've been takin' Chase out there since we moved to the Fort, and by now he's more familiar than I am with the woods, the paths, and hell just the land. He's a good kid, always respected the fact that it was a privilege to be invited, never took nothin' for granted. I fuckin ' love that boy, you know?

So yesterday PBJ called and he's got a surprise for Gar-boy. Told me to bring him out. I rounded my boys up, gave the old lady a kiss, and we headed off to the wilds of rural Indiana. Fuck, if these people had grown up in Kentucky, they'd know how laughable it is to call a little copse of trees ' the woods'. *Wilds my ass.*

I pulled up behind the barn, and PBJ's dogs are goin' off like they normally do, barkin' up a racket to alert anyone within a half a mile about the intruders. PBJ met us by the truck, and we shot the shit for a minute while the boys ran along the fence lines makin' friends with the pups.

We walked to the barn and I the instant I saw what PBJ had I rolled my eyes. "First person you thought of was me? Really?" He laughed, holding his hand out as if to ward me off. "Fucker. Boy's already after his own bike, this'll just make him crazier."

Two dirt bikes sat on their kickstands in the shadows. One significantly smaller than the other, but with similar paint jobs and handlebars.

"I got 'em from Red," he said, mentioning a Chicago brother who'd been patched into the club for a long time. "He upgraded and didn't have room to keep these."

"So you had to go and get 'em?" I shook my head. "Boys are gonna love 'em, you know it. Rocketing up to favorite uncle spot no doubt." I twisted and yelled out the doorway. "Chase, Gar-boy, come see what Uncle PBJ's got for you."

Chase already knew how to ride, of course. Since he'd come to me the boy'd grown up on the back of bikes, and had taken to it like a duck to water once I gave him the go ahead by buyin' a little 250cc for him. Garrett was too small yet for even that size bike, so he'd been relegated to riding with daddy, regardless how he pleaded.

My boys came running in, Chase in the process of pretending to lose a footrace to his younger brother. Loved when he did shit like that. Shit that he never had in his life before, but knew instinctively to give it to his little brother and sister. Chase's face lit up and he yelled a huge kind of 'wahoo' yodel, makin' PBJ grin wide.

Gar stood there staring at the smaller bike. He took a step towards it and paused, then looked back at me. I gave him a nod and he got within touching distance. Fuck man, his little hand was trembling when he reached out and laid his fingers on the grip. Without turning around, without the normal little-boy lisp he usually spoke with, he asked, "Is this for me?"

I nodded at PBJ, who told him, "Yeah, Gar-boy. That one's for you."

God, the look on that boy's face when he turned around, like he was about to burst, hope and love and pride and pleasure beaming from him.

Moments like that? They make everything worth it. All the sacrifices and time it took me to get to where I am today. My woman, my kids? Gettin' to see PBJ teach Garrett how to ride, with Chase watching on, making sure his little brother is safe and happy?

Fuckin' worth everything.

Worth even takin' Willa's wrath when we finally got home, dirty and skinned up from dumpin' the bike so many times. My woman wasn't well pleased that I hadn't told her what we were doing.

Not because she didn't want the boys riding.

No, my woman was pissed because she wanted to be there in the middle of the dirt and sweat, playing with the bikes and ridin' through the woods. I had to promise her we'd go out next weekend.

Won't be a hardship.

So fuckin' blessed.

MASON'S MUSINGS

#2

MARIALISA DEMORA

Facebook Group
Blog entry

A Good Man

This blog post of Mason's falls after Hoss, book #7 in the RWMC series.

Mason

Mornin'. Hope you're havin' a fine mornin' at your house, wherever you are.

I love all my brothers, and that's truth spoken. Each of 'em have earned my loyalty a thousand times over. Some of 'em are special to me, and there's something to be said about bein' brothers with a man like Jase.

Most outside folks know him best as a kickass hockey god. Well, at least to hear the man tell it. Makes me laugh, because while he did play hockey, and did it very well, that's such a fuckin' limiting thing to hold up as the be-all, end-all for him.

Him and DeeDee were here a couple weeks ago, our women chatting about everything from what book they were reading to what woman would get a rose on some fuckin' TV show. Kids were runnin' through the house like wild things that occasionally stopped in the middle of the grownups, vibrating to a stop as they asked for snacks, or drinks, or the code for Chase's game system--those were a yes, yes, and hell no, in case you're wondering.

Did you know DeeDee ain't her real name? That's a different story, though. See what I did there? Keep you comin' back for more. I'm relatively smarticle, as Willa likes to tell me.

So the kids are runnin' rampant and all of a sudden Gilda stops short and stares at me. "What, honey?" I wasn't sure what she needed, and the easiest way to keep her movin' was to figure it out.

"You're a nice man." She dragged her toe along the rug, acting shy like she does. She's real shy with outsiders, less so with the brothers, and I've known the child since she wasn't even in school, so I took this as a put-on to get attention. You know?

"Thanks, darlin'. You're pretty nice yourself." I reached out to give her hair a ruffle and she fuckin' flinched away from my hand. This wasn't a 'don't touch me because I'm shy' flinch, her moving away was accompanied by a look of sheer terror on her face. "*Jase*." That was all I had to say, because I knew from the vibe comin' off him, he'd seen it too.

"On it." He stood and scooped her up, and they disappeared into the kitchen for a few minutes. Next thing I heard was a loud, angry call for his old lady. "*DeeDee*."

She went, and stayed, and Jase stalked back into the room. Alone. Telling, yeah?

"Ride with me, brother."

No questions from me, my brother needed me so I stood and kissed Willa, then followed him outside. Twenty minutes later we pulled to the curb and killed our engines in front of a small house in a rundown neighborhood, set far back off the street. There was a school bus parked next to it.

Jase--or in this case, Captain, because in this moment he wasn't the hockey player, wasn't the kids' coach. No, this was my brother--fought for control before he started talking, the expression twisting his face tormented in a way I hated seeing. He lifted a hand and pointed at the little cottage. "Man in that house drives the bus takes the kids to school." I sat on my bike, waiting. "He watched as a boy touched my girl." I held my breath. "Happened this week. She sits on the seat right behind the driver, because she's so shy. This junior high boy sits up there next to her Monday, made her feel grownup. Then he touched her. Didn't hurt her, but he touched her in a way he shouldn't have." His voice was vibrating. "Man in that house told him to stop. The boy did." Captain was silent for a moment, then gave me the rest of it. "But the man in that house did not report it. I had to hear it from my little girl tonight, her sittin' on the counter in your kitchen, cryin' as she asked me why I was mad."

When we stood up and swung off our bikes, it was in unison. As was every other act that evening.

Man in that house was reported to the school district the next day, and subsequently fired after video footage backed up what Gilda said happened.

Man in that house stopped breathing the week after that, victim of a random break-in, and me? I didn't question a damn thing.

People think hockey is all Jase is or did. No, man. He's a brother, but more than that he's a father, don't matter those kids aren't his blood. They're his.

Jase'll do anything to protect his family. A good man.

One of the reasons I like the bastard so much.

HARDDRIVE HOLIDAYS

#7.5

MARIALISA DEMORA

DEDICATION

Dedicated to those of us who need a reminder that when you love, truly love, it is never too late to reconcile. Be open to possibilities that surround you, always ready to accept blessings, regardless of origin.

HARDDRIVE HOLIDAYS

Visited by the ghosts of Christmas past, can Harddrive find his way to the sweetest meaning of the holidays?

The holidays can be a joyous time, but when you have experienced a profound loss, they can also be filled with bittersweet memories. Take a trip down memory lane with a colorful, old-school biker, Landon Shoemaker, known throughout an active network of motorcycle shops and clubs as Harddrive.

With a long history twisted round with the Rebel Wayfarers, he has known Davis Mason since before there was a RWMC. Catch sight of the world our Rebels inhabit, seen through the filtering lens of an outside perspective, as Landon recognizes that family extends far beyond blood, and learns how well forgiveness can heal when it flows both ways.

ACKNOWLEDGMENTS

Ever since we first met Harddrive way back in *Slate*, I've been wondering exactly what his role was within the series. We saw his easy way with the customers in his shop, and witnessed his patience with Andy as they worked their way through an afternoon of bike shopping. Both of those things gave me a sense that the man was good, and I believed he was a biker in the way it was intended to be. Hard and unyielding, but passionate about the scoots. He was not a metro-corporate motorcycle riding man who claimed the title of biker, Harddrive just *WAS* one, living the life.

Then in *Gunny*, the man surfaced again, unnamed, but I knew it was him. He's the one who found the fork for the Vincent that Gunny was working on, only asking for a photo in payment. All about the scoots, man.

Finally, in *Mason*, I learned for certain that the Indian motorcycle Slate was so proud of had indeed once belonged to Mason. Full circle. Kinda like life. Like Erin would tell us, it was "Karma, baby."

But, it wasn't until *Hoss* when I for sure knew so much more of his story. When I learned that Dixie, my favorite bartender in the whole world, was his girl. That's when Harddrive got underneath my skin, and had to work his way out and onto the page to give me peace.

So, here you go. This is Harddrive's story, filled with so much loss and pain given through complicated misunderstandings, and him owning the decision every single day to not pick up that phone. Owning, and hating it, even as he believed he was doing the right thing.

I hope you enjoy reading the story half as much as I did discovering it. Muuwah. Big kisses to all of you, and a very Merry Christmas. <3

Woofully yours,

~ML (2015)

Harddrive Holidays

Living Large

Landon Shoemaker sat in his favorite chair, which was positioned the perfect distance between the heat radiating from the hearth's brightly blazing fire, and that damn chill that always settled nearer the log walls of his house this time of year. Relaxed in a way that working men understood, he had put in a good bit of work today and earned himself a good rest. Lifting the bottle held in his hand to his lips, he drank deeply, the yeasty overtones of the beer not registering as he sat, staring at the flickering flames through watering eyes.

Christmas Eve.

No celebration tonight, he thought, glancing over to where the Christmas tree had stood in past seasons, his lips twitching sideways in disappointment as he stared at the empty corner for a long minute. Hard to believe the year had slipped away from him again, but here he sat, on his own. The sole surviving member of his generation.

No family in the house. Back in the early part of the year, he had buried his brother, Rodney. His sister, Isabel...well, she had been gone for a long time. Gone long before she died, even. He had family left, products of his marriage, but his kids and their children were off living on their own in Billings and Fort Wayne. Not that he begrudged them their choices, but on a night like tonight, he would give a lot to see them crowding around the fireplace. To watch the grandkids rip brightly colored paper off boxes, their faces shining as they shouted with laughter.

He turned slightly, cutting a glance towards the matching chair next to his; both still pulled up in the middle of the room and angled so any occupants could easily carry on a conversation. That glance stuck on the empty seat for a long minute, and then he finally turned back to the fire and sighed. *No anything tonight.*

No kids meant no reason to decorate, so there was no holiday clutter anywhere in the room. No shine of glitter, no scent of evergreen. Hell, anymore, he did all his shopping online and simply had things shipped directly to his kids and grandkids, so he didn't even have any presents stacked and ready to distribute.

Lifting the bottle again, he took another drink. *No one to play Santa for*. He grinned crookedly at the rueful memories. Wars had been waged in this very room over who would wear the enormous red and white hat on Christmas Eves in the past, the winner granted rights over distribution of the presents. The expression slowly faded from his face as he thought of the stocking cap folded and still stored securely in the box of decorations up in the attic.

Shifting restlessly in the chair, he rolled his neck, listening to the tendons creak and make snapping noises. Stiff and tired, he was feeling his years tonight after working all day. The day before Christmas in Wyoming, you wouldn't expect people to be out doing their shopping at a bike store, but regardless of the forecast, the snow held off and shoppers had come in today in droves.

His store in Cheyenne sold bikes, gear, and parts for most of the major domestic brands of motorcycles, and a few foreign ones, too. His salespeople had worked the floor while he watched from his vantage point through the lofted office's window, grinning as the shirts and jackets fairly flew out the door. They had sold dozens of various chrome accessories, and he smirked now to think about it. One good thing about the brands he sold was seldom dealing with post-holiday returns, unlike some other stores. Enthusiasts enjoyed owning the best, and it was a point of pride for him to cater to that.

He yawned wide, his jaw cracking much as his neck had, and then he snorted a laugh when his belly joined in, growling loudly. Mentally composing a list, he went through the contents of his refrigerator, discarding various supper ideas until he reached the same conclusion he normally did when finally considering eating about this time of night. Pushing on the arms of the chair, he jackknifed to his feet, declaring to the empty room, "Cereal it is."

When his wife was here, she would have had his head for considering breakfast cereal a meal, but she hadn't been here for a long time, not for years. He swallowed, his throat suddenly tight, remembering the Christmas Eve dinners she would put on the table. Simple fare, but good, and always accompanied by a mug of her spiced rum, served with a sweet kiss.

It took some effort, but he pushed those thoughts aside.

Walking around the island that divided the kitchen from the rest of the open plan room, he made quick work of preparing his bowl, then leaned a hip against the front of the sink and ate standing, as was his custom these days. Gaze focused outward, staring through the dark panes of glass, he saw the snow the forecasters promised for Christmas had finally started falling. Tomorrow morning would find a fresh coat of white; pristine, it would patiently wait for kids with new winter gear to ski and sled. Their eager and tireless legs creating new tracks through the snow; those tracks plotting lines of experiences they would carry with them for the rest of their lives. Memories built to last.

Rinsing the empty bowl and putting it into the strainer, he turned from the window and his gaze swept the room. Mentally weighing the benefits of sleeping in what would at first be a very chilly bed versus the already warm recliner, he slowly made his way back to the chair, grabbing a hand-knitted afghan off the back of the couch on his way past. Dumping the covering on the seat, he quickly settled a couple of fresh logs on the fire, adjusting the existing fuel before putting the screen in place. Back in the chair, he draped the blanket across his legs, and then pushed the chair back, settling in and getting comfortable. Soon, the only sounds in the room were the crackle of the burning logs and the soft, deep breaths of the man sleeping in the chair.

"Rodney," he yelled, waiting for his older brother to catch up, nose pressed to the large window overlooking the sidewalk on which he stood. "Come on, slowpoke. Look at this, would ya?" The two brothers stood side-by-side in identical poses of excitement and admiration. "Would ya look at this," he said again, slowly, hearing the expected noise of approval from beside him.

They were staring into the car dealership where one of the salesmen had just rolled one of the biggest and prettiest motorcycles he had ever seen right in front of the wide picture window. The bike was shiny, so shiny he thought he could comb his hair using the reflection from the gas tank, and the salesman was using a handkerchief to polish the backs of the already gleaming mirrors. "Did you ever see anything like it?" Rodney asked, and he shook his head.

"Boys," he heard, and both he and Rodney automatically took a half-step back, because this voice belonged to the owner of the dealership. They both knew firsthand that he didn't like smudges on his windows, but instead of the expected scolding, the man asked them, "Do you boys want to come inside and get a good look at the motorcycle?"

Twisting, Landon looked up at the man whose big belly was doing a poor job of hiding behind his buttoned suit coat and nodded, answering for both of them. "You boys can help me out. I need a picture of someone on the bike for my newspaper advertisement. Let us see if you boys will fit the bill."

For the next thirty minutes, he and Rodney were in second Heaven after the man lifted and placed them astraddle the bike's seat, leaving them there while the photographer fiddled with his camera and lights. Landon even got to lean far forward, putting his hands on the straight handlebars, making vroom noises and pretending to drive the big bike. He had reverently touched the logo attached to the side of the gas tank, the headdress on the Indian man's head bumpy underneath the pad of his finger. Rodney played with the fringe on the bottom of the seat and the photographer took several pictures of them, the bright flash attached to his camera momentarily blinding the boys each time.

Landon shifted in the chair and looked owlishly around, blinking as if startled by something. With a sigh, he settled back into the chair, drifting back into sleep.

Delores stood in the space between the motorcycle and the porch of her parent's house, looking back at him with her fingers resting on her lips. She lifted and held them in front of her mouth, pretending to blow him a kiss. He reached up, catching it from the air and pressed his hand to his heart. Watching her walk inside he sat for another moment, waiting for the front porch light to be extinguished. Once the light was off and darkness had crept in around the small house, he kicked the bike to life, carefully walking the vehicle backwards out of the gravel driveway.

Riding back to Cheyenne in the dark, he thought back over the songs she had chosen to play on the jukebox at the diner tonight. Keeping his eyes on the cone of light stretching out in front of the bike, the headlight illuminated the lonely road as he sang his favorites loud and long. Pulling up behind the garage where he worked, he parked the bike underneath the stairs that led to his apartment. Stepping off the machine, he stretched with a groan and then trotted up those stairs, still humming under his breath. He had decided tonight, with her sitting beside him, hand in his, he was going to marry her. She was it for him and being with her gave him every feeling he had ever wanted.

Opening the door, he saw the envelope that had been pushed underneath onto the floor and stooped to pick it up. There was an official looking seal in the corner, but no postage stamp. He ripped the letter open, letting the envelope flutter to the floor as he read the words that would change the course of his life. "You are hereby directed to present yourself for Armed Forces Physical Examination..."

Dropping slowly into the upright chair near the door, he ran his hand across his face. Drafted. He had been drafted. He wasn't opposed to serving his country, not at all. This was exciting, and he wanted to share this moment with Delores. He knew her parents wouldn't look kindly on him roaring back into their driveway at this time of night, but he just couldn't hold it in until morning.

Rodney was already overseas, an enlisted soldier in the Army. Their parents had passed away several years ago, and Isabel...well, she was wherever she was, which wasn't here.

That left only one person he could think of that he could talk to, one person he could count on no matter what. Back straight, he jerked to his feet and looked around the apartment, thinking that everything now looked different, changed. Or at least it should. He had been drafted. A soldier.

Slamming the door shut behind him as he ran back outside, he shoved the letter into the pocket of his jacket, started the bike and recklessly pulled back out onto the road.

Driving fast and hard back to his hometown, he slid the bike to a stop in front of his best friend's home a little after two in the morning.

There were still lights on in Mike's house, and he suddenly wondered if he was the only one who had gotten news. Running up the back steps as he had a million times over the years, Landon burst into the kitchen to find Mike and his parents gathered around their kitchen table. They were all three somber-faced, sitting with what looked like a copy of the same letter he had received resting on the table between them.

Breathlessly, his voice filled with equal parts fear and excitement, he asked, "LeRoy, you too?" Mike nodded, and Landon sank into one of the chairs at the table.

No one spoke for a long time, and then lifting his chin, the senior LeRoy said, "Proud of both of you. This is not a small thing; it is a life-altering moment. Our boys, going over to the hellhole that is Vietnam. You gotta make sure you come back whole, come back to us. That means you'll need to watch each other's backs, become brothers in every way that matters."

A dog barking in the distance woke him, and he sat up, throwing the afghan to one side as he rose to tend the fire. Standing in front of the window again, he drank a glass of cold water, watching the snow falling outside. The wind had picked up and was pushing the white stuff around, drifts beginning to build around the bases of the trees in the yard. He tried to remember how much they were supposed to get, but couldn't put a figure on it. Six inches or two feet, the depth didn't matter since the store was closed tomorrow.

Vietnam. He hadn't thought about those years in a long time. After basic training, he and Mike had wound up in the same Navy unit and as Mike's father had requested, the already good friends became inseparable. He had come back from overseas after four long years to find Delores had married the local pharmacist, a man who hadn't been drafted because his skills were needed back home. They had three kids, and by all accounts, lived happy lives together still.

He grinned because Delores hadn't been the one for him after all. He should have realized that when one of his first thoughts upon being drafted was to talk to Mike, not caring enough to brave her parents and their potential wrath. No, the woman for him wasn't Delores, and he was damn glad he had figured it out. It had been Erin who knocked him for a loop, stole his heart. He sighed, thinking, *Holds it still to this day*.

Erin had walked into his life not long after he had gotten home and he fell for her in a big way. Strolling into the shop beside her big brother, she had walked around, fingertips grazing across the sleeves of the shirts on the rack. He was close enough to hear her soft hum when she touched the leather jackets, and that sound did it for him. He was a goner. He grinned again, thinking, *A goner with a boner*, because hearing the sound she made in the back of her throat gave him a stiffy every time.

Daily, for about a year, he asked her to be his wife. He would show up at the lunch counter where she worked, buying sodas he didn't drink just so he could talk to her. Every day her reason to refuse was different, some of them downright hilarious, saying things like she couldn't accept on any day that ended in a "Y." As the days and weeks crept onwards, he finally realized she was enjoying the wooing as much as he did, the sweetly-worded rejections her way of stretching things out. He grinned now, thinking about how she made him work for that yes, but it was work he had been happy to do; Erin out in front of him, a worthy prize at the end of the path showing him every day that she was worth it.

They did everything together, every minute that wasn't required at work, he spent by her side. There were bike rides and drive-in movies, Stampede Days parties and Sunday church with her folks. He kept plugging away at what he wanted until he finally wore down her resistance and she gave in. He thought people over in Billings might have heard his shouts of happiness when she finally turned her sweet lips his way, whispering the word he had so hoped to hear. LeRoy had been his best man, standing up at the front of the church with him as he watched his beauty walking up the aisle to put her hand in his. He sighed, looking over at her chair, frowning at the still-empty state. Always empty these days. He missed his wife.

Sitting in the chair, he stared at the fire for a time and then reached over, picking up his current read. Tipping the recliner seat back, he propped it in his lap and looked through several pages of the hardcover book, laughing at the captions listed underneath the black and white pictures of motorcycles and men, grinning at the faces of the ones he knew. Chuckling at all the things the writer had gotten wrong, he idly flipped back through the pages and then let the book fall shut. Tucking the peusdo-documentary into the chair beside him, he thought about all the men he had met over the years, the ones who ran through his shop, in and out within moments of days, and then he thought about the ones who stayed in his life. Closing his eyes, he slowly relaxed again, not even knowing when he drifted back down into sleep.

"Hey, honey. Look, Harddrive, that kid's back." Erin called him using his road name, and he walked to the front of the show floor, peering through the windows and across the highway. Sure enough, the wiry boy was standing and staring at the building, leaning against the same old, beat up pickup he usually drove. About once a month, the kid would come and park, standing and staring at their shop for a time before he would climb back into the truck and drive away.

"Come on, kid," he muttered. "Come on in. Give it up, boy. Why don't you come on inside here, come talk to me. Come and tell me what you need, son." After a moment, he hooted, yelling back at Erin, "Hot damn, baby, here he comes." The kid was walking across the highway, head on a swivel trying to inventory the line of bikes parked in front of the building. This was the kind of thing he lived for, the privilege of turning someone on to the lifestyle and the scoots. He had a feeling about this kid. You didn't come back again and again like he had been without having something calling to you. He loved sharing his passion for the bikes with people who gave a shit and from what he had seen, he suspected this kid would definitely give a shit.

Nearly two hours later, Landon was about out of tricks, having gone through his entire inventory of new bikes and most of the used ones without seeing anything other than polite interest on the kid's face. He had found out the kid was named Andy and was from a little town just north of Cheyenne where he lived with his grandparents some of the time. He had a nice egg saved up, expected to pay cash for whatever he bought, which meant this kid had been working for a while with this as a goal. Eying Erin's silhouette in the big window, he grinned. He could appreciate a man with a goal.

Harddrive walked them around to the back of the shop, where the rougher bikes were stored. These were the ones that had plenty of road miles on them before being traded in, and there wasn't a new model in the bunch, but it was what he had left. He had virtually given up finding anything when he suddenly saw it. *That interested spark he had been looking for. To test it, he deliberately passed over the bike the kid had his eyes fixed on, and saw the look of displeasure flash across Andy's face when he realized what Harddrive had done.*

Circling back to the red and white Indian, he remembered with fondness the day that particular scoot had rolled onto the lot. Nearly exactly like the one in the framed picture of him and Rodney back when they were eleven and twelve, the bike had come in underneath one of the roughest looking dudes Landon had ever seen.

This guy had looked like he spent half his life sitting on a motorcycle, and he handled the Indian like he breathed, totally by instinct...light and free, without having to match thoughts to deeds. But, in contrast to how he rode, the dude had carried a burden of worry that you could almost touch, it was that heavy. Mason, he had called himself, and then when they were filling out the paperwork Harddrive had found out it actually was the dude's name. Davis Mason, an officer in the Rebel Fiends out of Chicago, had traded in the aged bike on a much newer, more popular brand. Motoring off at the end of the day with a shit-eating grin on his face, ass on a growling monster of chrome and steel, leaving behind the Indian for the next owner.

Cheyenne wasn't a biker town per se, but there were enough clubs around town that he knew what a decent club looked and sounded like. He had asked around, and the young man who traded in the Indian was a better than decent guy. He was just a guy who had gotten hooked up with assholes, and needed to get away from them in the worst way.

Harddrive heard a few years later that Mason had been successful in extricating himself, and had started his own club. From all accounts, he did right by his members, which wouldn't surprise anyone who knew him, since he had lived through the shit his previous president had pulled.

These days, all the clubs in town knew of Mason and his Rebel Wayfarers, a club whose reach seemed to be growing every day. It was a pleasure to sell this bike, from that man to this kid, more especially when he felt the same vibes from Andy that he had Mason. Full circle, or as Erin would tell him, 'Karma.' He helped Andy load the bike into the back of that beater truck, strapping it down tight, talking through the process of unloading. When he handed over the jacket Andy had bought, he felt the pockets bulging and knew Erin had been at work, gifting the kid with goggles and gloves to round out his wardrobe.

She walked up, wrapping her arm around his waist as they watched the truck pull out, headed north. "You done good, old man," she said, digging her fingers into his ribs to make him squirm. She tipped her head back for a kiss and he obliged her, deepening the caress and wrapping his arms around her. "Wanna fuck?" she asked playfully when he pulled back and he grinned.

Before swooping back in for another kiss, he threw his head back and shouted into the shop, "All you motherfuckers need to get the hell outta Dodge and my shop, because I got a needy old lady who wants to get her some good time lovin'."

There was good-natured laughter all around, and when he raised his head from hers again, they were alone in the shop. One of the men leaving had even turned the sign over to Closed. He lifted Erin in his arms and carried her up to the office overlooking the sales floor, her holding on tight, their gazes locked. Setting one knee on the couch, he laid her back on the cushions and watched avidly as she pulled her loose-fitting shirt over her head, exposing her bare tits. He leaned in, cupping one with a palm as he covered the other with his mouth, pulling at her nipple with his teeth. His name rolled from her lips as she raised up, offering herself to him. "Harddrive."

Waking with a start, he sat up in the chair, looking around. Standing abruptly, he walked up the short hallway to the bedroom, a shiver running over him as his sock feet hit the floor, which was much colder this far away from the fire. Opening the bedroom doors one by one, he glanced inside, the moon reflecting on the snow so brightly he didn't need to turn on lights to know every room was empty. *Damn*, he thought, *I could have sworn I heard Erin.*

Back in the great room, he looked at the clock on the mantle to realize it was nearly three in the morning. "Fuck," he said, his shoulders dropping, "you ain't gonna be worth anything at work tomorrow, dirtbag." Then he snorted, muttering, "Oh, yeah. Christmas Day, fucking shop's closed."

Settling back into his chair, he fussed with the book for a minute, then draped the afghan across his legs again, tucking it underneath his thighs against the inescapable chill invading the room. "Shoulda just gone to bed, the fucking mattress would be warm by now," he grumbled to himself, half turning onto one hip and stretching his neck out. Eyes closed, he listened to the logs shifting as they burned, lulled back into sleep by the quiet noises in the house.

"Beautiful mama," he said, leaning in close for a kiss. "Love you, honey. Love you. Your mom is going to bring Barry to the hospital to see you and our pretty Dixie. You up for some kiddo chaos?"

Erin lifted her head, meeting his mouth with a smack. "You know it, baby." She grinned, exhaustion from the hours spent laboring to deliver their second child lining her face, but what shone clearest was her happiness. "I'm in little boy withdrawals, need me a fix." Cupping one hand around the back of his neck, she pulled him down for another kiss. "Or I could get me a fix of my big boy."

"Shameless huzzy," Harddrive groaned, kissing her hard and deep, cupping one breast through the shapeless drape the hospital offered patients. Tweaking her nipple, he pulled back when she laughed against his mouth. "What?"

"I'm leaking." She giggled and he looked down to see a growing patch of wetness around the nipple he had been fondling. "Go get our daughter, let's see if she'll latch on."

Walking back into her room with baby Dixie, he stood holding her until Erin had arranged herself, exposing one breast before she accepted the pink wrapped bundle into her arms. Settling their daughter against her chest, she smiled and leaned her head back on the pillow when the child began nursing.

"Beautiful mama," he whispered again, and then from his position on the bed beside her rested his cheek on her shoulder. He watched as she cupped the back of Dixie's head, fingertips stroking through the cap of dark hair their girl had been born with. "Love you, Erin. Love of my life," he said and she kissed his cheek.

"Thank you," she said softly and he pulled his gaze away from the sight of her cradling the life they created together, looking into her face. She lifted her other hand, cupping his cheek in the same way she held their daughter's head. "First you, then a boy, now a girl. My family is complete, Landon. Love you so much, old man. My happy ending."

He woke with a sigh this time, the sweetness of that memory cut through with the pain that his wife wasn't by his side anymore. "Fuck," he muttered, "stupid old man."

Standing, he moved the screen and jiggled the logs in the fire, settling them more securely and creating a cradle for new wood. Reaching in with the fresh fuel, he set the logs into place, using the poker to ensure they were secure. Putting the screen back in front of the fire, he stretched as he stood, looking around the room with a scowl. Pictures of his family seemed to mock him, the timeline of their history marching across the walls.

There was one of their wedding day, her draped across his lap on the bike in her short white dress, arms thrown around his neck as he kissed her. The picture froze them in place, his hand modestly on her waist. But, he could remember the shouts and catcalls of the men gathered around them as his hand raised from that position to cup her breast, her giggling into his mouth the whole time as she bent her knee and hooked her calf around his back, holding onto him as he held onto her.

Taking her back to the apartment over the shop, loving her sweet and slow, fucking her with both his eyes open, so he wouldn't miss a moment of her. Moving her into that same apartment, where she quickly turned the single room efficiency into a cozy home, filled with the personality of the woman he loved.

He looked at the picture for the grand reopening of the shop under the new name, Harddrive's Bikes and Gear. It was one of his favorites. Even though he had argued against the expense of hiring a photographer at the time, now he was glad for Erin's foresight. He loved it because the picture showed them standing, arms around each other, looking up at the signage with nearly identical grins. Right after that picture he had picked her up and swung them in a circle, her squealing the whole time about her skirt.

It wasn't until later he found out that her concern wasn't for folks seeing her panties, but because she hadn't been wearing any. That night, in their much larger apartment over the store, he had threatened to take her panties off with his teeth. That statement had been greeted by peals of laughter as she stood on top of the mattress in front of him. Playfully inching the full skirt up her thighs, she teasingly flashed her bare pussy at him with a grin before jumping off the bed on the other side, initiating what turned out to be an extremely short game of keep away.

That had been the night he planted their son in her womb, his body raised over hers on arms that trembled with fatigue and strain. He loved watching her when she found that place while he was deep inside her, so he stayed up and over her until she did. Leaning down to nip at her breast, feeling her fingers thread through his hair, guiding him to the other nipple where he licked and twirled around it with his tongue. So fucking good together, she wrapped him up with her arms and legs, fucking him back as she climaxed hard. "My woman," he had grunted, thrusting deep and holding as he came, groaning, his cock jerking inside her.

Reaching down, he adjusted his hardening cock, because thinking of fucking or making love to Erin always had that effect on him. He hadn't been with a woman since she left because no one else held a candle to her in his eyes. He knew from their mutual friends that she hadn't moved on either, and at least once a day he thought about calling her but never had the courage. The fear of what she would say weighed heavily on him because when things went sideways for them, they did so in a painful way.

Climbing back into his chair, he pulled one heel up onto the cushion, resting his wrist on top of his bent knee. Mindlessly snapping his fingers as he watched the flames, he sighed. Glancing back up at the pictures, he could trace the growth of their children, Barry and Dixie; looking at kindergarten class shots next to photos of the kids on their dirt bikes, arranged beside holiday and family dinner pictures, winding up with graduation. Their breakup hadn't come until after all of that, and because the pictures were her thing, they abruptly stopped right before Barry got married and Dixie moved away.

Stretching out his leg, he leaned back in the chair, flipping the blanket over his legs once again. *Damn woman*, he thought.

"You sure this is what you want, darlin'?" Staring at his daughter, he waited for her answer. That damn quick smile flashed on her face, full lips a legacy of her mother as Dixie nodded. He frowned, shaking his head. "Damn far away, baby girl. He won't stay around here instead?"

"Daddy," she scolded, reaching out to lift his hand and thread her fingers between his. "You know Keith's work is based out of Indiana. He was just up here for a job." She shrugged, squeezing his hand. "I love him. He's got to go back home, and I want to go with him."

"What did your mama say, Dix?" He tried to ignore the hurt that came with that question because it was another hit to his heart, acknowledging Erin wasn't living with him anymore.

"She told me to follow my heart," Dixie said softly, eyes on his face, concern evident on her features. "I wish I weren't going before you and Mom patched things up."

He pulled his hand back, making an abrupt movement. Turning his head, he looked out the window and could feel the scowl that settled on his face, brows pulling together painfully. "Don't let our troubles stop you from finding your happy, darlin'." He sighed, and then turned to look at his daughter, forcing a smile on his face. "We'll either settle our shit or we won't. You gotta live your life, and your mama's right, you gotta follow what feels right. If Keith feels right, if this is the path you're settled on, then you have my blessing. Love you, baby girl, so much."

"You never told me what happened—" she stopped when he made a noise. They stared at each other for a minute, and then she shook her head. "Alright, Daddy, but you know I love you, too." She stood and moved toward him, crawling onto his lap as he wrapped his arms around her, something he knew she had seen her mother do all her life.

"Baby girl," he whispered, pressing his lips to the side of her head, the pain from missing Erin compounded by the knowledge his daughter was leaving.

He lay there staring at a ceiling he could barely make out in the light reflected through the windows, having rolled onto his back during this sleep cycle. That memory was from nearly twenty years ago, and to this day he had never told either of their kids what happened. Stupid argument over nothing, escalating to a disaster of his own making because he was too fucking hardheaded to explain or apologize. "And not a day goes by that you don't fucking regret it, old man." His mutter was loud in the silence that draped through the house. "Fucking ghosts of the past, coming to visit on the eve of the holiday that started it all."

Shifting he looked at the fire, decided it was good enough for now and turned to his other hip, letting himself roll back down the hill into sleep.

"What was the one thing I've always told you I could never forgive?" The question whipped his head around and he stood looking at his wife, his hand on the arm of a woman attempting to straighten her clothing as she leaned one shoulder against the wall. Erin advanced toward him, placing one slow and careful foot in front of the other. "The only thing I asked you for, and you can't manage that one thing."

"Erin, baby—" he started but stopped when she shook her head, hair flying around her face, the ends nearly snapping with the violence of her movement.

"I've looked the other way when the boys around the shop danced with other partners, keeping my mouth shut so the only way their spouses and old ladies would find out was on their own. But, I told you, Landon. I said it and I meant it. If you stepped out on me, if you dipped your wick into a different well, then we would be done." She swept her hand towards the woman who stood there silently, eyes wide, head swiveling between the two people in the hallway with her. "This is our son's wedding, Landon. Quite the statement you've made."

Erin had always been stubborn, and she was mad enough that anything he said now would only make things worse, so he stood there, mouth closed, biting back the words he wanted to spit at her because it wasn't what it looked like. But, he could tell from the look on her face she wouldn't hear him, even if he said the words. And, even if she did hear him, she wouldn't believe him because he had laughed about the boys fucking around, joined in the randy joking about their escapades outside of their marital vows.

She turned on her heel and stalked back up the hallway, pausing at the end for a moment and turning to look at him. "I'll keep my mouth shut for Barry's sake because this is his day. But, I'll be sleeping elsewhere tonight, and tomorrow I'll come get my clothes. You keep everything, old man. I don't want anything to remind me of your cheating ass." She turned the corner and was gone, silence flooding in to fill the space behind her departure.

"Shit," the woman said softly, eyeing him with a shocked expression on her face.

"Yeah," he answered, not looking away from where he last saw Erin.

"You want me to tell her what happened?" Her voice was softly sorrowful because this was a fucked up situation if ever there was one. Unwanted, Erin's brother Angus had been rubbing up on this chick, leaving his wife sitting and waiting for him at their table at the wedding reception, and her not one speck wiser. Harddrive had run off his brother-in-law and then stayed to make sure the woman was okay. That was what Erin had walked into, not the tail end of him getting a taste of strange.

"She wouldn't believe you," he said curtly. Turning to look at her, he asked, "You okay?" She nodded and he sighed. "Might be a good idea if you left," he suggested and she nodded again. "You need me to find you a ride?" Wordlessly she shook her head and he had his turn nodding. "Take care," he said, turning to walk up the hallway, shivering as he passed the place Erin stood when she first started speaking.

"Fuck." He yelled this, waking with a start. Every fucking time he dreamed about that night, he fought to turn things, struggled in the hope that he could change the outcome, but wasn't ever able. It played out the way it had in real life, the last words Erin spoke to him scored in his brain. A nightmare. Sure, he could have called, but dammit, she should have known he would never do that, never fuck around on her. For twenty-three years, he had thought about picking up that fucking phone every single damn day.

"She could have called, too," he muttered, shifting his ass to one side as he drifted back to sleep.

"Papa." A soft voice called his name, and then there was a little body climbing into his lap. Wrapping his arms around the warm child, he blew out a deep, relaxing breath. "Papa Shoe, you're squishing me," the giggle came from underneath his chin, and he grinned, not wanting to wake from this dream.

"Shhhh." That whisper came from nearby, the voice tantalizing familiar. "Let Papa Shoe rest. Why don't you nap with him?" Shifting around, he pulled the now slack body against his side and let sleep roll over him again.

"Dad, I think we need to expand. Billings is a good market, and it would give me a chance to make a difference in a way I don't think I can in Cheyenne. You have the trade sewn up here, but Billings is an opportunity to look forward. We can shift the track the business is heading down, expand things, get into custom bikes." Shifting foot to foot, Barry stood in the kitchen of the log house he and Erin had built, the house their kids had grown up in. "I already found a building, and Gunny's

got me hooked up with a wicked talented mechanic. HBG2, what do you say?"

Looking at his son, his heart swelled with pride at the confidence his boy showed by bringing this to him. He knew that since Erin had left him, he had developed a bit of a reputation of being a hard-ass.

All the local cops knew him because his bar fights were the stuff legends were made of, so much that they dreaded seeing him pull into the local biker bar. More than once he was allowed to sleep off a drunk in the empty apartment over the shop instead of being taken to the local jail, mostly because even LEO didn't want to deal with him. For Barry to brave his shitty attitude showed balls.

"I think you're full of shit," he said and watched the muscles all along Barry's jaw jump as he clenched his teeth tightly, anticipating his father's next words. Harddrive was happy to disappoint for once and grinned broadly. "But I like the particular brand of crap you're selling. Grab a chair, let's get comfortable, sort out this opportunity."

By the end of the day, they had hammered out a tentative business plan and timeline, and that was the beginning of their expansion. Beginning with one new shop in Billings, Barry first made that location a success. He put in long hours and worked like a dog to make sure things were all handled in a way that shone the best possible light on them. Customer service issues were few and far between, and now they had expanded further, opening shops in Sturgis, Omaha, and Denver. Five stores, all of them profitable, because of his son's hard work.

Barry had called him a couple weeks before Thanksgiving this year, talking about heading further south, maybe looking at New Mexico for their next shop. The key in every location was getting the right mechanics and managers in place. Mason and several of his Rebels had proven instrumental in giving them leads on good men and women. He had proven to be a good friend to have in many ways.

As a good club should be, the Rebel club membership was far more like family than friends, and Harddrive had been humbled and honored at the sendoff the club had given Rodney when he passed from lung cancer several months ago.

Harddrive's brother had slipped into the life after Vietnam, too. Rolling wild and crazy through his days, never settling in any one place for long, at least not until he found the Rebels. He took a road name, Bingo, but had never taken an old lady, claiming his poetry was a jealous bitch. That man could string words together in a way that surprised Harddrive every time he listened to one of those poems read aloud. There were commemorative signs on the wall of every shop with lines from Rodney's work etched into them, words and plaques set in place on the day each store opened. It was a way for him to have his brother with him, no matter where Bingo rolled.

Having Mason be involved in the club his brother was in proved interesting, and lucrative. Between the friendship he had with Mason, and the brothers Bingo had in the club, the Rebels called Barry for a hell of a lot of bike-related purchases. It seemed they were shipping parts across the country nearly every week, and he would never admit it to Barry, but it meant his damned, pain-in-the-ass computer inventory was a benefit. The kid had good ideas and kept pushing him into adopting things that hadn't even been thought of when he opened the first shop.

Then he got a call from Bingo, telling him their sister had shown up in Fort Wayne, stoned out of her gourd, with a half-dozen kids in tow. They had both lost touch with her years before, back when her relationship decisions put the family at risk. She had left town with that deadbeat boyfriend, dropping out of sight along with five thousand dollars of their parent's savings.

After reconnecting with Bingo, over the next few years, she popped out three more kids, the dads never staying in the picture for long. Then he got another phone call because Bingo found out she got cancer. Mother of nine, her body worn to pieces by life and the disease.

Bingo had been living in Chicago at the time, patched into the Rebel's mother chapter, but Mason gave him the go ahead to charter a new one in Fort Wayne. Named him president and gave him the chance to run things there. Gave him an opportunity to be there for Isabel, try and ease her way. It wasn't long before they buried her, and Harddrive had made his first trip to the Fort, as the locals affectionately called the town.

There he had heard stories about Andy; finding out the kid had stumbled into Mason's bar in Chicago years before, still riding the Indian motorcycle Harddrive had sold him. The same one that Mason had traded in years before that. Now called Slate, the kid wasn't a kid anymore, and the word through the grapevine was his experiences during his travels were writ large on his skin. Twisted and good, his life seemed wound up in Mason and the Rebels, both coming and going.

Then came a call from Mason. Bingo was in the hospital, diagnosis lung cancer, the prognosis grim. He made the trip to the Fort again, flying in this time because he wanted to ensure he got there before Rodney went under the knife. He had very nearly picked up the phone that night, stalking in restless circles around the hospital waiting room, the desire to hear Erin's voice ricocheting through his head like a pinball machine gone insane.

A hard and shitty thing to have to go through alone and Mason had known this, sending men down to wait with him. Bear and Gunny were there, already known to him because of their passion for building and restoring motorcycles. He had met Hoss and Road Runner, an interesting pair of men because, like Bingo, they shared a creative bent, Hoss a painter and Road creating art out of food as a chef.

Bingo came through that surgery okay, and before he returned to Wyoming, Harddrive saw him set-up in a home with a couple who seemed determined to adopt the man and their sister's kids. Bingo had taken responsibility for the rug rats when their sister died, circling those peewees with love and support, making a good life for all of them. Harddrive watched the care Jase and DeeDee took with his brother and it eased his mind considerably when he had to go home, knowing that even if he was traveling down a hard road, Bingo was surrounded by people who loved him.

Then came the final call. A conversation he had expected, but dreaded. He and Barry headed out immediately, riding into Fort Wayne two days after getting word that Bingo had died. He hadn't been thinking sensibly when he left, or he would probably have taken the truck instead of the bike, because once he got into the wind and had a minute to quiet his mind he realized he would need to bring the kids home with him. Then, after arriving in Fort Wayne, he found things were rather different than he expected because that same couple who had loved on Bingo wanted to take on the entire passel of Shoemaker kids in a permanent way.

He found himself relieved he didn't have to uproot the kiddos, because they had been through so much in their young lives. He was determined to be a big part of their growing up from here out. He made arrangements to keep an open line to Jase and DeeDee, laying plans to talk to them and the kids every week. Those few days had been filled with reunions and memories, as he and people who knew Bingo shared recollections and stories about the man.

Dixie and Keith came to the wake at the Rebel clubhouse the night before the funeral. He had watched with pride as the men of the club treated her with great respect, knowing that came from them knowing the goodness of her heart, and the commitment of her old man.

Then his mood had soured when he saw Angus, his wife's brother, standing near the bar inside the clubhouse. That stupid, cheating motherfucker had always managed to land on his feet, and seeing him hooked up with Mason's crew only proved his lucky streak hadn't ended. Listening carefully, he heard the Rebel members calling Angus a different name, Pike. The man's road name was after a fucking fish, and Harddrive shook his head at how right someone had gotten that particular moniker.

After a few minutes, he decided to take the bull by the horns, forcing a meeting to keep from having awkwardness later. Slapping his hand on Pike's shoulder hard, he saw the startled fear chase across his face when he recognized Harddrive. "How the fuck are you?" Harddrive asked, his disbelieving gaze catching for a moment on the President patch on Pike's vest.

"Good, man. It's good to see you," Pike said, holding out his hand for a shake. His gut churning, he gripped the hand of the man who cost him his marriage, cost him decades of loneliness and pain. "Rodney was a good person, Landon, I was sure sorry to get the call."

Lifting his chin in response, fury rising to fill him, Harddrive stepped back and dropped his hands to his sides. Staring at the man in front of him, he opened his mouth, then clamped his lips closed, shaking his head before he turned away. He hadn't gotten two steps before a hand gripped his bicep, pulling him to a stop. He heard Pike's voice, soft in a way that would keep the words private. "I'm sorry, brother."

At that term coming out of that mouth, he jerked his arm out of the grip and whirled, staring into Pike's face. Spitting out the words, he asked, "Is it four or five marriages now? How many you ruin, man? I ain't your goddamned brother. *You saw to that. You know what? Why don't you stay the fuck away from me. You got nothing I need, and you sure don't have any condolences I'll believe." Stalking away, he saw Mason watching their exchange, a considering look on his face.*

Fortunately, those were the only words he had with the man, and the service the next day was conducted with all honor and respect. Then came the military gun salute, and the awarding of the flag. He had asked DeeDee to take it for safekeeping. The entire ritual was filled with moments when he wished like hell Erin was beside him. She and Rodney had been good friends, and she would have loved to see how he would be missed by these worthy people. He hoped like hell that one of their kids had thought to tell her about him passing.

Tears stood in his eyes as he held one of his nephews in his lap at the graveside, overwhelmed at the sheer number of people who had come to bid farewell to his brother. When one of Bingo's poems was read over the casket, it was all he could do to hold it together.

"Papa." The child's voice was complaining again. "I want to stay with Papa Shoe."

"Shhhh, baby." Now he recognized the voice for certain, knowing his Dixie-Girl had spoken from nearby, and he shivered briefly at the chill as his grandchild was lifted from his lap.

That chill didn't last long because his lap didn't remain empty.

Taking a deep breath, he smelled his wife's favorite perfume and felt a smile curl the corners of his mouth. Wrapping his arms around her, he held her tightly, nuzzling the top of her head as she sat with him like she had done so often, sharing the recliner in front of the fire. He reached down, pulling the blanket up and over her legs too, tugging it high on her shoulders. "What are you doing, old man?" He smiled at how well his imagination had filled in her voice, giving it a rasp and thickness he only heard when she was close to tears.

"It's cold out, Erin. I don't want you to get sick, baby," he said, slipping his arms underneath the blanket and wrapping them back around her. "God, I love you, baby," he whispered, feeling her fold herself against his chest like she always did. "Missed you every single fucking day." He swallowed hard, thinking to himself that he would be crying in his sleep next.

"I'm so sorry," she whispered, and he shook his head, but she kept talking to him. "Angus called, Landon. He told me—" she stopped when he shook his head again.

With a heavy sigh, he told his wife, "I could call you. Hell, I could tell you. Coulda told you a thousand times over the years. Wanted to, even. But, he's your big brother and he always took care of you as best he could. He's your blood, and I ain't gonna take that from you, Erin. I love you too much." He hugged her tightly, shifting in the chair. "I'm sorry, too. So much time gone, days we would never get back, gone." He kissed her forehead, smiling. "Lovin' this dream, old lady. Lovin' feeling you. Missed this so fucking much."

"Why is Mama Shoe crying?" *Damn, Dixie's boy is loud when he wants to be,* Harddrive thought, shifting in the chair again, the weight on his lap anchoring him in place, Erin's breath soft and warm on his neck as she nuzzled against him.

He froze, finally realizing that he wasn't asleep. His house was no longer silent, there were voices in the hallway where the bedrooms were, water running in the kitchen sink, and Keith cleared his throat over by the fireplace. "Mama Shoe's just happy," his son-in-law said, and Harddrive took a deep breath, pulling in the scent that always told him Erin was nearby. *My baby's home,* he thought, and took another experimental breath, finding the same intoxicating result.

Opening his eyes, he flicked his gaze at Keith, who stood by the fireplace with little Landon Junior in his arms, both of them looking at where Harddrive sat in the recliner. There was a decorated Christmas tree in the corner, the base piled high with colorfully wrapped boxes and bags. Evergreen draped the mantle, the pictures there carefully arranged amidst the greenery.

Barry walked into view, handing Keith a mug of what looked and smelled like coffee, his youngest daughter hanging onto his leg, her ass on the top of his foot as he shuffled along. Harddrive grinned, remembering the days when he would have a kid on each leg in exactly the same way.

Without moving his head, he peered down at his lap, gasping aloud when he saw Erin nestled against his chest, crookedly covered by the blanket he had pulled over them. Licking his lips, he started to speak, then swallowed hard, suddenly unsure of himself. This was what he had wanted every time he let himself dream, Erin back in their home, his arms, always in his heart. She fit into his lap as if no time had passed, the gray now threading through her hair not diminishing her beauty one bit. *God, I love her,* he thought, arms tightening around her. *My old lady.*

"Landon," she whispered, and he shushed her gently, stroking up and down her back, his hands memorizing the curves he remembered so well.

"Doesn't matter, baby. Not if you're back. If you're back, then my heart is healed." His eyes slipped closed, and he said, "Kiss me to seal the deal?" Her fingers fluttered along his jaw, drawing his face down to hers as she kissed him, her lips hot and demanding against his. Breaking away, he opened his eyes, staring down into her face, watching as she smiled with trembling lips. “Hell, yeah,” he said with a grin. “My old lady.” He took her mouth again, tasting her this time, loving the sounds she made in her throat. “Love you, baby. Merry Christmas, Erin.”

***

From my house to yours, I hope you have a very Merry Christmas!

~ML

BIKER CHICK CAMPOUT

MARIALISA DEMORA

DEDICATION

To my son, who amazes me every day with his capacity for love and life: Love ya, bubba.

BIKER CHICK CAMPOUT

The segregated circles in which motorcycle club princesses and prospective members travel seldom collide. When they do, if romance is involved, it can be an improbable match at best.

Carmela Estavez is tired. Tired of being the princess, she's had enough of never living up to family expectations, and she is seriously fed up with people watching her every move. Riding her motorcycle cross-country to meet up with friends, she's ditched her daddy-mandated escort and is ready to spread her wings and fly. She just hopes she doesn't crash and burn in the process.

Justin Youngblood has wanted to be a member of the Rebel Wayfarers MC for as long as he can remember. Hurley, as he's not-so-fondly known, is powering through his prospect period, but not always on the right side of his brothers in the club. This means that at nearly a year into his tryout, he's still getting slapped with the punishment details. This weekend is a perfect example, chaperoning a hen's party in the middle of nowhere that won't get him any points with anyone.

Then what looked to be a boring weekend turned into the ride of his life when in rolled a honey-skinned beauty. He's supposed to be on guard duty, not on the prowl, but there's just something about this one. She's got trouble written all over her, and if there's something he likes, it's getting into trouble.

Biker Chick Campout

Hurley

"You gotta be fuckin' *kiddin'* me." Justin Youngblood ground his teeth together in irritation when his brain belatedly caught up with his mouth, and he realized he'd spoken those words aloud. Snapping his lips shut on the mutter that was just barely underneath his breath, he froze in place, hoping no one had heard. Quickly tipping his chin down, he broke the stare he'd been directing towards his chapter president.

Not good. Not good, Justin's head supplied about five seconds too late. This was something he already knew because the vibe in the room had gotten heavy, the air thick, hard to breathe. That shit happened when you had fifteen pissed off alpha males in the same space. *Time for damage control*. "Sorry, brother. Respect. More than willing to do whatever's needed, Slate, but you sure I'm the one you want in that van?"

Justin had just been informed he would be the sole escort for a weekend bash some of the brothers' old ladies were planning. The timing sucked, because recent chatter across the entire club was about a possible rollout to Indy, and maybe beyond, depending on how things shook out. The call was expected any day, which meant if this bullshit assignment stuck to him, he would be in the woods on the western edge of the state and not in place to make a play.

And he needed to make a play.

Said play would be calculated so he'd be part of something important, the success of which would help solidify his place in the club. It had to be big. Bigger than this girls' night out party, for sure. He groused silently, *Get stuck with this, gonna be a fuckin' perpetual prospect. I need a real chance to show the club what I can do.*

Rebel Wayfarers MC were his family. A true family for him, and had been for years. But, things had stalled since he'd sewn on the prospect patch, and lately, it felt as if he was skirting a little farther away into the weeds instead of drawing closer to the inner circle. *One fuckin' chance, is that too much to ask?* Every major run the club dealt with seemed to happen when he wasn't around, and that kind of repeated slight looked intentional, which cemented his feelings.

He knew from the sympathetic looks turned his way he wasn't the only one under the impression the old guys were keeping him at arms-length. His instincts said those men still thought of him as the snot-nosed kid who'd been running around the clubhouses and garages since before he was old enough to grow a beard. He reached up, stroking across his cheeks, feeling the rough stubble of a five o'clock shadow. *Put the lie to that every day*, he thought, *now if the OGs would just pay goddamned attention to what's right in front of their faces*.

"*Prospect*." A warning growl whipped through the air, the curt tone drawing a stinging line down his ego, as intended. That would be Gunny, the member he most looked up to. A man who was mentoring him, bringing him along and making sure Justin didn't fuck up too badly. He'd given Justin his road name, too, after a particularly bad night of celebration. Not a name he'd expected—or liked at first—but regardless the origin, he'd embraced it in a way that made certain everyone understood his pride. "First, his *title* is president, not brother. When he tells you to do something, that's who's speaking. Second, and do not mistake this as being less important, Hurley, tell me you did not just disrespect our prez?"

"Unintentional, SAA." Hurley backpedaled, hating every second of moments like this because he knew it would look exactly like what it was: him trying to save face. A tactic to which he seemed to resort far too often. Gunny was the Fort's sergeant at arms, and he drilled protocol and rules into Hurley all the time. Just didn't seem to stick. "Respect, Gunny." *Gotta watch my alligator mouth*, he thought, feeling the eyes of every man in the room on him. Hurley consciously straightened his shoulders, standing taller, determined to pull every inch he owned into play. "If there's a need, I'm all over it."

"No shit, Sherlock? *Jesus*. You want my gratitude for givin' me that? *Fuck me*. Hurley, there's a need, or I wouldn't have fucking said I *needed* you to roll the van to Chi-town for a fuckin' pickup." Slate, the Fort Wayne chapter president and a man who wasn't Hurley's biggest fan, glared at him. Somehow between when Slate took over from Bingo here in the Fort four years ago, and nine months ago when Hurley patched into the club, he'd managed to run afoul of the man no less than a half a dozen times.

Slate glared across the bar to where Hurley stood. It was Hurley's night to serve as a waitress to club members. Not something he enjoyed, but an assignment was an assignment. *And that's how you need to look at this fuckin' campout*. An assignment. Nothing more, nothing less. Not any kind of a slur or dig; just another meaningless task to complete in his efforts to earn full membership in the club. Hurley swallowed, his mouth suddenly full of acid as the thought of failure loomed.

Shaking his head, Slate snapped, "Pros, you should know by now that I ain't gonna explain my fuckin' ass every fuckin' time I tell you something. I say it, you do it. It's a simple fuckin' exchange. What you don't do is bow up and get your panties in a twist every fuckin' time someone opens their goddamned mouth." Slate shook his head. "You're gonna have to bury that shit," he paused, and Hurley would understand why when the words he most dreaded were finally spoken, "or you ain't gonna make the cut, man."

Threat delivered, Slate stared at him. With difficulty, Hurley stood his ground and held Slate's gaze until the corners of his president's eyes crinkled, signaling Slate had moved past the moment and was sliding away from pissed. That was how Slate and most of the men in the club handled things. Once something was in the past, it was forgotten unless you fucked up again. *Until*, he corrected himself with an inward wince.

"DeeDee's sortin' all kinds of shit for the trip. Talk to her, let her know if she's bein' unreasonable." DeeDee was Slate's mother-in-law, and a long-time Rebel old lady, having been hooked up with one of the founders of the Fort Wayne chapter. Hurley remembered Winger fondly and was glad DeeDee had found herself a life after losing both her husband, and her daughter, Lockee, to an accident. She remained immersed in the club, managing one of the businesses, and was now old lady to a newer member, Captain. Without saying the words, Slate was telling him even if she was an RWOL, DeeDee wasn't in charge. This had the pleasant effect of giving Hurley a tiny sliver of his manhood back, even while acknowledging that she'd probably be busting his balls. *Hard*.

"You got it, Prez." Hurley tried to imbue the title with respect and love and brotherhood, all rolled into one, and knew his brother understood everything Hurley was trying to say when Slate stepped forward, reaching out. Hurley met his grip, letting himself be pulled into a clinch, careful to steer clear of the center patch on Slate's vest when he thumped with one fist. Not his place, not yet. Only patched members should handle the colors that every man worked his ass off to earn, and Hurley hadn't made it that far. *Not yet*.

Slate stepped back, and with a tip of his head called Gunny and the other officers through the door behind the bar. Business afoot no doubt, and Hurley stuck behind the fucking bar for the night.

Tomorrow he'd have a chat with DeeDee and see just how screwed he was gonna be on this little safari. Didn't matter what anyone said, he knew up front it wasn't going to be anywhere near worth his time, because sitting in a forest listening to the bitches play their games wasn't within spitting distance of anything he wanted to do. And with DeeDee, you never knew what to expect. He'd known her a long time, and she could be up for a lot of things. He'd suspected he'd get an inkling of her plans from whatever shopping list she'd thrown together, and then be able to sort out what he wanted to push back on from there.

"Pros." He heard his—*please God*—temporary title called and looked over at the pool tables to see a group of members looking his way. Worm, another of the many long-time members, that very longevity a tribute to the worth and value men found in the club, waggled an empty bottle his way, calling, "Beer, bitch." With a nod Hurley bent back to his tasks for the evening, pulling three bottles from the cooler stashed behind the bar and slipping a bottle opener from the back pocket of his jeans.

"On it, brother," he called.

***

"She's gonna try to piss you off, but don't let her get to you." That was DeeDee speaking from behind him as they wound their way through aisle after aisle of the grocery store. She'd laid claim to his assistance the minute Slate passed the word along, and the past couple of days it seemed all Hurley had time to do was tend to chick business and listen to her talk. Right now she was yammering on about Ruby, Slate's old lady, but she wasn't telling him anything he didn't already know. Slate's dislike of him had bled through to his woman, and Ruby expressed that dislike every chance she had. Vigorously.

DeeDee spoke again, still out of sight. “She’s been cooped up with the twins. ‘Course that’s her own fault, having four kids all in diapers at the same time.” Her tone changed, turned musing when she asked, “What was she thinking? Four kids that close together? Crazy momma.” A sigh, then she called out, “Hold on. Stop here, let me look.” Brushing past him as he rolled to a slow stop, she reached out to the shelves and grabbed a couple of cans, tossing them into the cart. “You just gotta hold your cool. Gotta let her do her thing, Hurley. She’ll burn out fast.”

Turning to look at him, the expression on DeeDee’s face softened as she registered his displeasure; she appeared almost regretful. “Don’t look like that, honey.” Carefully he blanked his features, wiping away the sneer he was sure he’d been wearing. “You know this is an honor, right?” She was another who had known him his whole life. Shit, he’d only stopped calling her Mama Dee a couple of years past. *No doubt she thinks it’s a fine assignment for a piddly little prospect.*

“Yeah, right. Sure I do.” Pushing past her, he leaned his forearms to the cart handle and continued up the aisle. “Where to next, DeeDee?” No sound of following footsteps so he paused and glanced back to see her still planted, unmoving. Rolling his eyes, he asked, “What?”

She stared at him for a long moment before stating firmly, “You know who I am. You know who Ruby is. You better have learned about Mica and the rest of the gals from Chicago by now, and I know the boys are long on history, so I trust you have. So how exactly do you see this as beneath you?" Head tipping to one side, she sighed heavily. "You see us as unimportant? We're just the old ladies, so no big. Ain't no thang, right?" He straightened and opened his mouth to speak, but DeeDee raised her voice, cutting him off.

"Club first, we all know that. Every woman who hooks her life and love to a man in a club gets where she stands. And she only stands there for as long as she remembers. Try to make a man choose, you might not like the choice he makes. But we women," —she gestured to herself— "we also know that we make your lives easier. We know that we matter. We know our men worry and fret, and the less reason we give them to do that, the more they can focus on staying healthy and making good decisions. Every time Slate or Jase roll out there's a chance they won't come back, and my job is to make it so they have one less thing to worry about. If you," —her hand swept out, not quite finger-pointing, but it was close— "think that's not worth your time, if you believe that making it so our men worry less is so far beneath you, then you should petition to stay at home. Us old ladies? Honey, we don't want you. Don't want you and sure as hell don't need you, except as our men feel you are necessary. You go on now, walk away," —hands to her hips, head tipped far to the other side— "I got this."

Shaking his head, he tipped his chin down as he told her, "You're a pain in my ass. When did you turn into a drama mama?"

"Isn't me pulling a drama in the middle of a grocery store." She denied her tirade, and he laughed, looking up to find her grinning at him. "Gonna help an old lady out?"

His answer was to ask, "What's next on your long-ass list of things to do?"

Carmela

Following the cone of her headlight through the deepening dusk, she guided the bike down the country road, steering carefully around the sweeps and curves. The bright light of a bonfire shone through the trunks of the trees lining the road, and she smiled at the sight. Navigating the final turn, she slowed to a crawl, dropping her feet to balance the bike as she braked to a stop. This was the first of what she hoped would be many annual girls' weekends, and she had been looking forward to having a chance to talk, really have conversations with the women she saw already gathered around the fire and camping spaces in the clearing ahead.

Heads had popped up at the sound of her engine, and she mentally counted off the women, putting names to faces as they appeared. Standing next to two bikes near a partially erected tent was DeeDee Spencer, a longtime biker babe from Fort Wayne. In a space adjacent to her stood a petite blonde and a striking black woman, Jessica Nalan, and her girlfriend, Brandy Still. It looked like those two had ridden down together on Brandy's cherry red crotch rocket. Opening the bike's throttle a little, she continued rounding the clearing in a broad sweep, pulling up next to three bikes parked in a neat row. These would belong to the other women from Chicago, Mica Rupert, her sister Molly Scott, and their friend Kathy Montcell.

Carmela Estavez shifted into neutral and then carefully pushed her bike backwards onto the concrete pad, toeing down the kickstand and killing the engine before she tipped the bike over onto the support. Taking off her jacket, she folded and draped it over her handlebars, rolling her wrists and stretching out her forearms. Looking around, with a broad, welcoming smile she nodded at the women coming her way. *"Hola, mi amigas,"* she called happily, lifting her leg over the seat just in time to be engulfed in a hug from first one, then another of the women. Passed rapidly from one set of arms to another, she found herself finally at rest, tucked into a lean body, and she looked up, grinning. "DeeDee," she said, "so happy to see you, mama."

One hand smoothing her hair, she heard DeeDee say, "Good to see you, too, honey. We were starting to worry when you weren't here by sundown."

"Give her to me." This shout came from behind her, and she turned in DeeDee's arms, knowing to whom that voice belonged. Headed her direction was a determined-looking redhead. Carmela twisted, holding out her arms in welcome, as they wrapped each other up in a hug. When the affectionate greeting came, it was soft as a wish. "Maria Luisa Carmela Estavez, I'm so glad you were able to come."

"Ruby Melanie Davidson Jones." Her own voice was rough with emotion. "I'm so glad I could make it, too." She stepped back, her hands dropping to Ruby's wrists, holding on to that connection. "Lookin' good, little mama. Who knew popping out two babies at a time would make you even more beautiful. Oh yeah, baby. You'll find out if you look this good with four kids, your old man's gonna keep you busy-busy, *chica*."

"Shut up, Mela," Ruby scoffed, pulling her in for another hug. "I've missed you, missed talking to you. College agrees with you, it looks like." The diminutive woman dropped one hand and turned, towing Carmela behind her across the clearing, and so didn't see the change Carmela knew came over her face. She was glad Ruby didn't see her expression of anger and frustration because having her friend know everything that had been going on would only cast a pall on their time together, and even before leaving for this trip, she had been determined not to let anything ruin the weekend.

Oblivious to her brooding thoughts, Ruby kept babbling, dragging her along in her wake. "Everyone's already here and unpacked. Supper first, then we can set up your tent. Food's ready, and we're just about to eat, so let's get you some pre-grub libations."

Turning around to scan the open space, she saw a van nearby parked nearly underneath the trees, out of the way. "Whose cage?" she asked, following Ruby.

The eye roll was nearly audible when Ruby responded, "Slate had one of our prospects drive it. The pros is under strict orders from me to not leave the interior." She giggled. "Hurley is a nice guy, but this is girls' weekend. I'm glad he was able to bring the coolers and chairs, but we don't need no dicks all up in our business."

"Says the woman who's getting regular dick up in her business, as is evidenced by the beautiful babies she keeps producing." Carmela laughed, throwing herself onto a blanket spread near a grouping of lounge chairs. Looking around at the tents and chairs, she asked, "Seriously? How much shit did you guys bring? Are you truly going to make the poor boy stay in the van all weekend? Does he at least have some titty magazines to keep him busy?" She had winced when Ruby said he wasn't allowed out of the vehicle because, after the last two months, she hated being the reason for anyone to have less than free rein of their own wishes.

"Ewwww. I don't want to think about how Hurley would get busy in that van. I have to drive it sometimes." This came from Kathy, and as she turned to sit in one of the lawn chairs Carmela saw the back of the leather vest she wore over her sweater.

"Ohhh, Kathy. Did you finally get patched? How long did it take you to convince him, all of two minutes?" She accepted a red plastic cup full of wine from Ruby, stretching her legs out on the blanket with a sigh. It had been a long couple of days, and she had ridden hard to make it here in time. "Digger, right?" Kathy had been enamored with a handsome, tall, shy biker from Chicago for a while, but the last Carmela heard they weren't that serious. Things had apparently changed because her wearing a 'Property of Digger' patch on her vest was a declaration of an ownership that went both ways.

"Yeah." Kathy went quiet for a moment, accepting her own cup from DeeDee. She lifted her head and looked around at the women. "It means a lot that he wants me." The smile on her face was filled with undiluted pleasure, knowing in this group she would never receive criticism for welcoming a role that people on the outside might look on with disdain, not understanding what the words actually meant.

Carmela looked around, listening as everyone chipped in, confidently explaining to Kathy how lucky Digger was to have her. They were good friends, from varied backgrounds, but having the most important thing in common: all of them had at least one foot in the motorcycle club life. A life that some people romanticized, but here, among these women, she knew every one of them understood what it took to be part of, yet apart from the things that impacted their family and friends.

Except for her, every woman here held an affiliation with the Rebel Wayfarers, from either the Chicago or Fort Wayne chapters. Some of them, like DeeDee, Ruby, and Kathy, were in relationships with men who belonged to the club. Mica, Molly, Jess, and Brandy were friends of the club, attached in less definite ways, but still part of their extended family.

As usual, I'm the odd one out, she thought, taking a deep drink. She was associated with the Rebel club by friendship, one that was long-lasting and profound, but not actually part of this family. Hers lay far to the west, with one part in Mexico where the Machos, her father's club, was based and the second part in Las Cruces, New Mexico, where she lived with a family associated with yet another club, the Southern Soldiers.

"Hurley can come out to eat now, but that's it. Afterwards, he will be banished again. Banished to the nether regions of the van." Ruby got her attention with another giggle and Carmela looked at her, head tilted.

"You already drunk, woman? When did you start sucking wine back? Yesterday?" She took another deep drink. "Pansy-ass shit, shouldn't be hitting you that hard." She glanced at Ruby again, then turned and yelled. "Mica, where's the fucking tequila?"

"Now you're talking," Mica shouted from across the fire pit, and before Carmela knew what was happening, all the women were standing, holding smaller plastic cups while the dark-haired woman freely poured liquor in each. Holding the bottle by the neck, she lifted it and tapped it against each cup's rim. "To us, the baddest women in town." With a laughter-filled chorus of 'fuck yeah' and 'you know it,' the women all raised their cups and drank.

"Brats are done," DeeDee said a minute later, leaning sideways to escape the heat of the fire as she turned the bratwurst sizzling on the campfire grill. "Ruby, get out the slaw. Mica, did you say you packed some chips? Wanna grab those and the plates for me?" She turned to look around, "Brandy, I know you had Hurley drop by to pick up dessert, so you're off the hook for anything else."

As the food and other things were brought out and organized, Carmela turned to DeeDee. "I'll go let the poor boy know he can come make a plate. I still can't believe you're making him stay in the van."

DeeDee leaned close and whispered, her voice shaking with laughter, "I can't believe he's letting us."

Picking up her tequila cup, Carmela let Mica top her off with another inch or so of the clear liquor, thanking her with a grin. *God, I love these women*, she thought. Carmela had been away from home at college until recently when events around the Southern Soldiers had warranted enough concern for her father to force her withdrawal. Since then she had been locked away in their compound, not permitted to even go grocery shopping in town.

Of course, this trip had been forbidden, but she had ridden off anyway, knowing her father would order men after her. That was why she was late to the gathering today, having barely evaded yet another friendly snare set for her, hearing the dismayed and angry shouts from above as she passed underneath a bridge on a small country road. She knew it would be miles before her father's men could exit the highway they were on, and by that time, she was long gone, making up for lost time on the final portion of her ride.

She settled, leaning against the side of the van and listening to the playful shouts from her friends. Watching the gathered women in the light from the fire, seeing how their faces glowed against the darkness, Jess running wild through the group; it felt as if she were observing delight and joy in motion. Flickering flames cast a luminous glow across them, contrasting against the dark shadows forming along the edges of the encircling trees. Those shadows larger than life, beaten back by the light's embracing arms stretching wide to promise support and love.

Lost in her thoughts, she didn't realize for a minute there had been no movement from within the van. Her weight against the side had rocked it in place, which should have announced to the occupant that he had a visitor. With a sigh, she shifted the cup to her other hand, stretching out her arm to quietly knock on the door.

After a couple more minutes with no answering movement or noise from inside the vehicle, she knocked again, slightly louder. Same non-result. "Oh for fuck's sake," she sighed, "I'm hungry." Twisting to open the door, she called, "Hello the van" —the panel moving soundlessly as it glided through the grooves— "it's time to rise and shine" —smiling in expectation of surprised questions— "sleeping beauty." The interior lights remained dark, either disconnected or burned out, leaving only the light from the fire to illuminate the inside of the vehicle. Her gaze dropped, seeing a man asleep, stretched out on a thin mattress. A threadbare sheet twisted low around his legs his only cover, leaving most of his naked body on display.

"*Madre de Dios*," she whispered, her gaze drifting slowly from his face to his body, down to the juncture of his thighs, then back up to his face. He was beautiful. There was no other word for it, the man was beautiful. Even in the uncertain light, she could see his hair was long and blond; it looked sun-bleached, slightly curly where the ends escaped from a rude ponytail, carelessly tied back with a leather thong. His face was handsomely symmetrical, arched eyebrows over almond shaped eyes, sharp cheekbones, and a square chin.

He had attractive black and gray half-sleeve tattoos, and on the shoulder facing her, she saw a *Dia de los Muertos* sugar skull, inked with impressive detail. His arms and body were sleekly muscled, not bulked outlandishly, but toned in a way that let you know he was strong because he worked for a living, not a gym rat. Trailing her gaze lower, she let her eyes linger there for a moment, studying where his soft, but still impressive cock curled in a bed of dark blond hair.

He didn't move, didn't react, but his stillness subtly changed in a way that brought her gaze back to his face, mortified to find his eyes now open and staring at *her*. With a silent groan, she turned away, giving him her back. "*Dios lo siento!* I'm so sorry," she muttered, feeling her cheeks blazing with embarrassment. "I was...I mean I meant...came to...wanted..." *Puta mierda*, she thought, *pull it together, Mela*. "Dinner's ready." Rattled, she finally got her words out, discomfited even more by hearing him moving around behind her, probably pulling jeans up those long, muscled thighs...*Mela*, she scolded herself, *he's a prospect, no matter how fine. He would never look at you that way.*

Hurley

You gotta be fucking kidding me. Hurley barely kept his mouth shut as the girl ogling him whipped around, turning and giving him her back. Just a girl; not an old lady, surely. She was mature enough to consider a woman, but only just, even if she had curves for days. *Jesus*. Where she stood framed in the open door, the firelight cast a halo around her, letting him pick out all the enticing places on her body that so fascinated him at first glance.

He'd woken as soon as the van's door opened, an initial thrill of fear following him up out of his dreams. Had feigned sleep to try and evaluate the situation, and instead of a threat…found her. So Hurley lay still and observed, enjoying watching her look at him, eating him up with her eyes before she realized he was aware. He'd savored the unguarded expression of raw hunger that played across her face, and even now his cock would be willing to stand up and salute her.

Worn jeans cinched tight at her waist, that soft fabric covering every inch of her south of those luscious hips. *Bet with an ass like that, she never lacks for attention*. She'd have an old man, must have, given the company in the clearing beyond where she stood. *Doesn't matter how much she looked at the merchandise. Never mind what she might have been thinking, ain't no way a sweet piece like that is for me, not if she's here with this crew*. The stumbling apology she'd given was cute, and he knew if she didn't have that gorgeous brown skin, there'd be a fiery-red blush racing up her cheeks.

Bitch ain't for me. Hurley reached down, giving himself one slow, firm stroke before abandoning the grip on his hard cock. *Man can dream, though.* And he would tonight, would be doing some hard dreaming while lying on the paltry mattress that Ruby threw at him before she basically locked him in the van.

Gotta find a way to get that woman to let up on me, he thought as he dressed, laying his leather vest near the door. That symbol of everything he wanted was heavier now than it had been a week ago, because in giving him this honor—and that was how he'd tried to look at it, at least after his dressing down—Slate had also handed him a center patch, bringing him more officially into the fold. *Fucking finally.* Missing a bottom rocker yet, but that would come in time.

His eyes trailed across the form of the woman still with her back to him, and he allowed himself a moment to dream right then. Good woman on the back of his bike, a solid chick. The one he chose would *get* the club and the life in a way that meant he wouldn't have to explain everything to her.

A woman like the ones going crazy, dancing around the bonfire; real women. An old lady, a partner, someone he could lean on. The honey-skinned beauty in front of him was the perfect example of what he'd be looking for. A woman not afraid of her own appetites—he grunted when his cock began to fatten, his flagging erection rekindling—or his. Strong, not a weak flower that needed protecting. Like DeeDee told him, a woman who understood the life would have her man's back in every way she could.

He let his gaze trace this woman's body again, lingering on those hips. Shapely as they were, it was as if those curves were calling for his hands to grip and pull. Hold on tight, riding hard as he wanted. A woman like this one, stacked and full-figured, she could take some rough handling. A dream worth having. She shifted, and he saw the delicate angles of her features, eyes a dark shimmer glimpsed only from the side as she resolutely kept her face averted. Could take anything, but God…he'd give her the world if she were his old lady. *My old lady will be my queen*.

Hurley shook himself, scooting to the edge of the opening as he dropped his boots out the door. *Not ready for that yet*, he thought, *need to pay attention to business*. Get that rocker. Get solid in the club, make it so every brother knew he had their six, no matter what. Only then could he start looking for his queen. *Man can dream, though*.

Carmela

Two hands settled on her shoulders, and she nearly shrieked at the unexpected touch. They gently moved her sideways a step, fingertips trailing softly down the slopes of her shoulders and upper arms. "Okay," he said, and as soon as she heard it, she immediately thought his voice was beautiful, too. That single spoken word caused her to shiver, and she felt gooseflesh rise all along her arms in response. He asked, "Need anything from inside the van?" She turned to look at him and became mesmerized, watching him slip socked feet into boots. *So beautiful*, she thought. He finished and sat on the edge of the doorway looking up at her for a moment. He had put on jeans, but no shirt and she could see the dark swirls of those tattoos on his upper arms. "Well?"

Startled, she must have looked as confused as she felt because he laughed softly, corners of his mouth curling up slightly before asking a second time, "Need anything from inside the van?" That laugh caused the same kind of shiver to flow through her, and this time, she felt a clenching low in her belly. Shaking her head, she answered him wordlessly, not confident she could still speak. Most of her thoughts were jumbled, the only coherent ones to do, again, with his beauty. *How could someone so beautiful be called Hurley*, she mused, then shook her head, not caring, because the evidence was right in front of her. "Got that in one, doll." She must have looked confused because he laughed. "You already said 'no,' honey."

"Oh," she forced out, trying to mask her embarrassment by lifting the cup of tequila and taking a drink. *Dios, he must think I'm an idiot*, she thought.

"Whatcha got?" he asked and reached out, casually plucking the cup from her grip. Sniffing, he made a face and turned his head sideways, then lifted the cup and sipped. He made a rough noise in the back of his throat as he lowered the cup, then raised it and sipped again. "Mica's good stuff," he said with a grin, passing her the cup back. "I have my own stash I don't tell her about. If she knew what I liked to drink, she'd lecture me about fermenting practices and aging properties."

"Umm hmm," she agreed, still watching his face. *Beautiful*.

"I'm Hurley." He gave her a chin lift, and then unfolded fluidly and stood next to her, so close she could feel the heat rolling off him. An intimate distance, one that could be eliminated if she swayed only the slightest amount. "I'm with the Rebels out of Fort Wayne, but they use me to slog shit here and there" —he swung an arm out, indicating the van behind them— "such as food and amenities for hen's parties in the middle of fucking nowhere."

Rolling her lips between her teeth, she clamped down on them and nodded. *Say something*, she thought. *You've been around men like him all your life. Why has this hermoso gringo stolen your voice, chica?*

"Normally when one person of a group or gathering introduces themselves, it's courteous for the other parties present to reciprocate," he said with another grin, this one sly, drawing his lips sideways as he openly teased her. "Let's try this again, honey. Hi there, I'm Hurley."

Cheeks blazing hot, she dropped her gaze to the ground. Forcing her mouth open, she took in a breath, and then murmured, "Mela." She cleared her throat. "I'm Mela. Carmela, actually, but my friends call me Mela. Like mellow, but with an aah sound. Mela."

She heard him move and saw his feet shift closer, that heat raging hotter all along her body, her awareness of him intensifying. A bold move, he wasn't making any effort to hide his interest. His voice deepened and grew husky as he let the sounds of her name roll off his tongue, "Mela." Darting a glance at him, she saw he was looking down at her with a soft smile on his face. "My pleasure, honey." His hand gripped hers and in an instant, the scene in front of her was gone and in the place of the beautiful young *gringo,* her mind showed her an older Mexican man. Angry, his hard, sweaty hands reaching out to grasp her wrists. It was only a moment until with a jolt, she jerked free and closed her eyes, opening them just in time to see Hurley take a step back, probably assuming her reaction was to his touch. Which it was, just not in the way he imagined. Not a rejection of him, but of her memories. "So..." —his voice trailed off uncertainly, then picked back up, the look on his face lost in the deepening shadows— "you said dinner was ready?"

She nodded and her movement seemed to be his exit cue. Before she could say anything else he had reached behind her, bringing out and putting on his cut. Then, carefully and obviously not touching her, he closed the van door before wordlessly turning and walking towards the fire. Away from her and her fears, leaving her standing alone.

Mela took a few minutes to collect herself before trailing him back to the group. Standing beside the bonfire, she accepted another slug of liquor and took a plate of food from Jess, who slipped in sideways for a quick hug. Hands full, Mela leaned into the gesture, both women laughing at the awkward embrace. Mela said, “Wasn’t sure if we’d see you and Brandy. I heard from Slate that her business is booming.”

Mouth full of food, Jess nodded wildly, then swallowed and grinned. “She’s doing so well, but I always knew she would. A Little piece of genius, my woman. Hooked my wagon to a rising star, ya know.” She paused for a moment and then, eyes darting back and forth between Mela and something behind her, gestured with a fake casualness as she asked, “So...what happened by the van?”

“Hmmm?” Mela lifted her plate and nibbled at the chips piled on the edge. Working one between her lips without the use of her hands, she grinned around it at Jess, and then, mouth still filled with chip, mumbled, “Wha chu mean?”

“Hurley came over here in a hurry like he was all manly he-man pissed off. I figured he tried to hit on you, and you swirled him. Boosh, down the drain.” Jess giggled and pretended to press a lever with her middle finger. “Salute...and...boosh, take your swirly, mister Hurley.”

Shaking her head, Mela opened her mouth but was interrupted by that same shiver-causing male voice. “She barged in and got an eyeful, then ice princessed on me, Jess. Middle of the summer and cold as fuck. I suspect my package didn’t meet inspection.” Turning, Mela saw Hurley had walked up behind them, bun-wrapped brat in one hand, and a beer in the other. "But maybe it was the label instead. Guess the lowly prospect never had a chance, huh, princess?"

God, she *hated* that term. Mela actually felt her chin tip towards her neck and knew a scowl had settled on her face. "Don't talk about what you don't know, pros," she said coldly, turning away.

"Ohh. Ice burn," Jess joked, sliding her arm back around Mela. Shuffling her feet, she turned them in a circle, laughing when they were again facing Hurley. Staring, he lifted his beer and drank, gaze never leaving her face. Mela's eyes dipped, and she glowered at the ground between them. A moment later she felt Jess' arm drop away and was puzzled when she heard Jess murmur, "Well, alrighty, then."

"So, enlighten me, princess." Hurley kept his voice quiet, apparently not intending anyone else to hear him when he asked, "Why'd you freeze up? Surely you've seen everything right? I'm not that hard to gawk at, am I?"

Looking up, she was again struck by how damned good-looking he was, even in the weak light of the fire. "You already know you're easy on the eyes, pros. I just didn't mean to burst in on you like that. Everyone deserves some privacy," she said, trying to match her tone to his. "I couldn't imagine how anyone could sleep through all the noise this crew was making, so I thought maybe you were sulking in there." She glanced around the clearing, feeling a half-smile curl her lips as she watched Jess drag Brandy into the space between their tent and the fire, pulling her girlfriend close to dance. *That girl.*

"It bothered me when they said you had to stay in the van," she admitted, glancing up to find him still watching her intently. "I just...I don't know..." she shrugged. "Wanted to tell you it was okay to come out. That you didn't have to. Stay in the van, you know? You were free to come and go as you please."

"And that really mattered to you." He sounded surprised, and she nodded. Shaking his head, he said, "As you've pointed out, I am only a lowly prospect."

"I didn't mean it like that," she lied and saw his chin come up.

"Yes you did, princess. I get it. Trust me, after the past year? I get it, putting me in my place." He turned and looked away from her, then glanced back. "Prospect is on my back, but the club is in my blood, and my name isn't prospect, it's Hurley."

She was silent for a moment. "I'm sorry." *For so much.* "For opening the van without making sure you were ready, and for insulting your standing in the club." *For making you feel less than you are.* "The Rebels trust you to keep their old ladies safe," she said, gesturing out at the groups of women sitting, dancing, or reclining on blankets talking. "That tells me you are more than 'just' anything to your club." Tipping her head towards her friend, she indicated Ruby. "Right there is your chapter president's woman, but more than that, she is his life, stolen from him once before. Something so precious, he guards her night and day. For him to entrust her to you means something." Turning to look at Mica and Molly, she directed his attention that way with a tilt of her head, then turned to gaze up at him. "I *know* what those two mean to your national president." His expression had become severe, the line of his jaw hardening as his gaze remained locked on her face, listening carefully to her words.

"Each of these women is important to someone in the club. Different chapters, but each of them your brother." Appetite vanished, she bent to place her plate on the ground, and then turned, looking outwards, towards the edge of the clearing. Into the darkness, out where the woods began. *Anything could be hiding in those woods*, she thought with a shiver. *Anyone*. "This is a secluded location. Nothing about us being here was publicized." She snorted softly before continuing, "Even Jess was warned off social media. But, even your national president clearly holds you in some esteem, because you are here" —she swept a hand out to indicate the women— "with all of them. Their lone protector for the weekend."

"I didn't really think about it like that." Hurley shook his head. "Should have, the guys laid it out for me. But, *Jesus*, all the politics that go along with prospecting into a club kinda muddies things." He scoffed. "Politics. They've had me doing double-time, shuffling between Chicago and the Fort. Most days it feels like double the pressure because I'm trying to please two chapters. It's almost more than I can wrap my head around sometimes." He fell silent, and she could see his shoulders contract in a protective move; he'd said more than he intended. He shifted his feet, boots shuffling in the grass, voice flat as he muttered, "I'll head back to the van. Thanks for the insight, Mela. Food for thought."

At her name coming from his lips, she drew a breath. "Wait," she blurted, and then paused, at a loss because she didn't know what she'd intended to say. She knew what she was feeling and had been for days. Angry and out-of-control, like she was free-falling all alone. Hurley helped quell those feelings, and she wasn't ready to lose that, even if it were something he didn't know he offered.

They stood like that for a moment, and then he tilted his head and held out a hand. Not overtly, so everyone would notice. No, his arm extended only slightly, a discrete angle of his palm towards her. His words wrapped around her, a slow cadence of exploration. "Wanna talk some more?" Without hesitation she reached out, accepting the invitation by slipping suddenly cold fingers into his warm ones, letting his large hand engulf hers, and following as he tugged, pulling her towards the shadows by the van. He opened the door, and they settled side by side in the opening, Mela shifting back far enough to bring her legs up, crossing them Indian-style, all while Hurley doggedly retained possession of her hand.

"I've never seen you around the clubhouses." He spoke quietly, threading and unthreading his fingers between hers, a constant caress of skin-on-skin. The non-question didn't surprise her because only a few people knew what her affiliations were. She shook her head. He continued, "If you aren't club, then why are you here?"

Lifting her gaze to him, she answered his question with one of her own. "Do you know the story of how Slate came to the Rebels, and how he got his name?" At his headshake, she drew a breath, and then told him, "It's one hell of a story. You should ask him about it sometime. How he came by his name, granted by his president on the day he first wore his own prospect patch." Lifting up her other hand, she held finger and thumb a hairsbreadth apart. "I factor into it in a small way, *muy poco*, very small. Tiny." She drew a breath that audibly shivered from her nerves, every word she spoke dancing along the borders of pain. *How far do I let him in?* "Everything happened so long ago, it seems nearly a dream sometimes. A nightmare, but so long ago I pray the edges are all worn and can no longer hurt me."

He made a noise and tugged at her hand until she turned to look at him, waiting for the questions she knew would come. "You know Slate well?" he asked, and she nodded.

"He saved me," she whispered, the simple words saying so much, the weight of gratitude in her heart expressed aloud.

They sat in silence for a minute, his thumb slowly stroking back and forth across her knuckles, then with words slow and cautious Hurley asked, "From what?"

Reminding herself she didn't know him, she shifted sideways and tugged, gently pulling her hand from his grasp, needing some separation. As she spoke, she fell into the formal cadence of one to whom English was a second language, reverting to the lessons of her youth, learned before she knew betrayal. Before fear and pain became constant companions. "From the time I was small, my father and uncle disagreed on many things about me. Over the years, their arguments escalated, raging out of control. Swirling around the family until I wound up in a dangerous place, surrounded by dangerous men."

She took a deep breath, dancing around the edges of truth. "Men who were there for business, of which I was a part. Before he met Mason, before he knew of the Rebels,

Slate," —she smiled, watching as Hurley's gaze grew more intent, eyes dipping to her lips, then back to her eyes— "who I still call Uncle Andy" —Hurley's eyes widened in surprise— "rode to the rescue of a frightened and impressionable young Mexican girl, one forced too quickly into adulthood.

"That is how I am connected to these women" —as she spoke she folded her hands in her lap, knowing her words sounded stilted, aloof. Distant, as if the things she endured had happened to another, that distance was something this story always demanded from her— "because while my association with the Rebels may have started with Slate, it continues through my friendship with his woman, Ruby," —she paused a moment— "and with Mason." Mela shook her head, so many things left unspoken even with everything she'd said. "Mason and my father have partnered together often in the past few years, and I hold a Rebel challenge coin, giving me free passage into or through any territory your club claims."

Digging into the front pocket of her jeans, she pulled out a coin. Just larger than a silver dollar, it was heavy and hot, the metal warm from resting so near her skin. Handing it to him, she watched as Hurley turned it back and forth, examining both sides of the thick disc, then Mela held out her hand to retrieve it. He placed it in her palm, his fingers trailing along hers in a sensual motion.

"Tell me how you came to be here?" Unnerved by his silence, affected by his touch, she had to firm her voice as she asked the question, pushing the treasured Rebel token back into her pocket. She wasn't sure if she would receive a real answer because some men came to a club through paths they preferred not to disclose. *Hurley is not one of those men*, she thought, as he spoke.

"Mom left Dad and me when I was about five," he began. "My dad's best friend was a Rebel. Well, he didn't start out a Rebel, but the president of their club folded it in years ago, so he got grandfathered in. Dad and Diablo, his friend, and Winger, the president, worked on bikes in Dad's garage until the Rebels bought it to run their own show. By then, I was working in the shop every day after school. Just wrenching, nothing fancy. Nothing at all like Bear can do. You know him? That man is amazing."

She murmured, "I've seen some of his work. Very nice." Bear and Diablo were names with which she was familiar, and Winger, married to DeeDee, was a man she had known well. Lockee, their daughter, had been only a little older than she was, so the two girls were thrown together whenever there was a meeting where families were invited. Winger and Lockee died several years ago in a car wreck, and it still shocked her to think that bright, vibrant Lockee would never grow older. Lockee would never meet and marry a man she loved, never bear his children. All the things any girl hoped to experience, now an impossibility.

"Yeah, nice is an understatement. Being around the guys made me realize that the club, being a member, was something I wanted. More than anything, I wanted it. Slate forced me to wait until I was legal to officially prospect in, but now I'm nearly at the nine-month mark, still going strong." In the darkness, she saw his silhouette move and then caught a glint from his teeth as he smiled.

"So you're twenty-one?" Mela was surprised at her disappointment at the revelation. She'd thought he was older. He both looked and acted more mature than most of the boys her own age.

"Twenty-two now," Hurley told her, that glint of smile shining at her again. "My birthday was yesterday."

"Seriously?" She shifted to sit upright and he moved with her, reaching out to place his palm on her back, supporting her confidently. "Your birthday was yesterday? That deserves some cake or something. Some kind of celebration." Heat spread through her from his touch, and impulsively she placed her hand on his forearm and leaned forward, intending to brush her lips across his cheek.

"Happy birth—" she began, interrupted when he turned his head and pressed his lips to hers. Her eyes dipped closed of their own volition, and her small gasp of surprise must have seemed an invitation because his mouth opened, velvet tongue boldly trailing across her bottom lip. The kiss ended slowly, Hurley pressing his lips to hers twice, gently working her mouth before sliding his cheek next to hers. *Bad idea*, she thought. *Very bad idea. Terrible idea.* Breathlessly she finished, "—day."

She felt the supporting arm slide further around her back as his other hand came up, sweeping the hair off her neck so he could dust kisses up the column of her throat. "Mmmm." The noise he made in the back of his throat was low and sexy, and she couldn't stop the shiver that rolled through her again. "Thank you," he murmured, kissing the hinge of her jaw— "for the" —moving back to nip her earlobe— "birthday" —lips back to her jaw, trailing along it as he kissed up to her mouth— "wishes."

The heat from his hands traveled up and down her arms, tingles of sensation trailing the path of his palms where they moved over her skin. Wanting more, she arched her neck, and he accepted the silent invitation, pressing hard, open-mouthed kisses along her jaw and back up to her mouth. This time, when his tongue teased along her lips, she opened to him, feeling that same shiver work its way up her spine as he swept into her mouth, possessing her in a way that made her wet between her legs. *Dios*. Desire curling in her belly, inner muscles clenching down on emptiness. Lips working, caressing her mouth, he tangled their tongues together, and she felt his hands shifting her closer as the kiss deepened, the taste of him flooding her senses.

Her hands were winding helplessly, one twisted in his shirt, trying to pull him closer, and the other twined in his hair, threading through and cupping the back of his head. *Want him*. Pulling him against her body demandingly, desperate for his touch. *Need this*. Plucking at the piece of leather tying his hair back, she released it, and his dark blond locks fell around them, creating a silky curtain that swayed with each movement.

The muscles of her stomach jolted and lurched with surprise as one of his hands slipped underneath her shirt, backs of his knuckles brushing along her ribs in a barely-there touch. He broke the kiss and pressed his lips to the side of her head, his breathing as ragged as hers when he said, "Mela, don't tell me to stop, please *God*." His hand rose along her ribs, thumb stroking the side of her breast and then across her already hard nipple, dragging roughly against the fabric of her bra. "Want you," he murmured, palming her breast and plumping it, slipping his fingers inside to tease her bare skin.

"Yes," she breathed, and he made an eager noise in response. Easing her back onto the mattress, he propped himself over her on an arm as he reached down, lifting and bringing her legs into the van. With one hand, he grasped the handle, and she watched the wedge of light from the fire grow smaller, narrowing and then finally winking out of existence as the door closed. Eyes stretched wide, adjusting to the darkness, she found just enough light filtered in through the windows to identify his silhouette where he knelt between her feet. From the tilt of his head, she thought he was looking down at her, so when she felt his hands on her ankles, she didn't jump.

Wordlessly he tugged her boots from her feet, chill night air stealing across her skin as he slipped her socks off and tucked them into each boot, setting the paired footwear aside. In the same fashion, he slowly, methodically undressed her. His focus on her was unsettling, but he seemed totally in control. Stretching his hands out, his fingers found and worked the fastening at the waistband of her jeans. Bending her knees, palms sliding in a firm motion down her hips, he removed them, taking her panties at the same time. She watched as he carefully laid her folded clothing next to her boots.

In silence he reached out to grab one of her hands and tugged, pulling her into a sitting position. Hands sliding around and under her shirt, he worked the fastener on her bra, and then took her shirt and bra off, discarding them next to the growing pile of clothes.

Totally nude, as she sat in front of him, waiting, she felt spotlighted in the limited light shining through the windows, her eagerness waning while the moments ticked past without him touching her. Nervously, she swallowed hard, then lifted and crossed her arms, hiding her stiffening nipples. *Too much, I can't—*

Mela was startled when Hurley said, voice low and forceful, "Don't cover yourself. Let me look at you." The command was clear, certainty infusing his tone. Dropping her arms, she still felt exposed and had to fight the urge to bring her knees up to her chest, but she wanted him so badly. *Dios*. Aroused, she was hesitant to do anything that would cause him to stop. In the end, desire won out over inhibition, and she sat in silence, legs curled in front of her, arms at her sides. "Fucking *gorgeous*," he said in that same greedy, possessive tone. He took a deep breath, and she found her chest rising in an echo of the movement. "Blinding me, you're so beautiful."

Moving slowly, he took off his cut, folding it carefully, each motion showing a deep respect for his club. Then with quick movements, he tossed his own clothing aside with far less care than he'd shown hers.

Lifting one hand, he swept his hair back from his face, releasing it as he tilted his head and then reached out to her, each of these actions seeming to take forever until the moment he finally touched her. With a firm grip, he cupped each foot, tugging her legs open, and pulling her down the mattress and towards him.

"Lie down, Mela," he said softly, running his hands up the inside of her legs and back down, his thumb stroking along the arch of each foot. "Lay back; let me make you feel good." Gentle caresses, each one stealing her breath. "Let me make it good for you, honey."

His reverent tone and the constant touches, soothing heat from his hands across her skin gave her the courage to do as he asked. His hands stroked higher across her ankles, then the inside of her knees, sweeping down, then up again, farther, then—*frustratingly*—back down. He moved and she was devastated, losing all contact with his hands. It was only a moment and then she cried out, unable to still the tremble that swept through her when his thumbs, palms, and fingertips again trailed up and down her skin. Delicious torture, because while she longed for each caress, she couldn't predict the path his hands would take, her keen anticipation overwhelming, keeping her on edge.

Rising on his knees, he bent over and then his mouth was on her, tracing a heated path up one inner thigh. His breath ghosting across her skin merely a prelude, leaving her gasping at the first bold swipe of his tongue across her intimate lips. With a moan, she lifted her hips, movement compelled by the sensation. Hurley chuckled, deliberate fingers leisurely gliding up and down the folds between her legs. Mela felt the smooth slide, the touch of his work-roughened hands glancing soft as spun silk through the evidence of her desire.

"God, honey," he muttered, lips brushing across the skin of her inner thigh as he spoke. "You're fucking drenched for me." She was. Had been since she opened the van door to feast her eyes on his beauty. With a shift in position, he lapped at her, the tip of his tongue teasing her clit out of its hood as he sucked that bundle of nerves into his mouth. Heat enveloped her, skin sensitized from each touch leaping at the sensations he rained upon her.

"Mmmm." He made that noise in the back of his throat again, and she shivered. "Fucking drenched. Love it, love the way you taste." His hands were touching and stroking, then she felt one finger slide inside her, heard the whine escape her lips at the sensation of being filled, but not full. *Need more.*

Moving slowly, steadily, he pushed deep, and his other fingers spread across her ass, gripping tightly as he thrust in, grinding hard. Then, he stroked out just as slowly, plunging back inside with two fingers, the more generous width stretching her. *God, yes.*

It sounded like a vow when he said, "Gonna make you feel good." One arm braced across her hips, holding her in place, he fell into a rhythm, his hand moving, fingers thrusting, hot mouth sucking. He laughed when she lost her grip on the sheet, demandingly threading one hand through his hair, and the vibration against her sex had her drawing her knees up and out, voluntarily opening for him. *Promise fulfilled.*

"God," he muttered, pressing his mouth against her, the movement and speed of his tongue and fingers increasing as he flicked and licked— "so good" —drilling inside and then sucking hard, each nuance of movement forcing her towards what felt like a dangerous precipice. "Fucking gorgeous." His words were nearly inaudible over the sounds of him going down on her, the noises her body made as it accepted every touch, and she realized she was making constant incoherent entreaties of desire and arousal. His fingers slid in and out fast, reaching inside, pumping, seeking as she clenched around him in pulses, waves of pleasure rolling closer. "Come for me, baby. Come on," he coaxed, lapping at her lips, fingers driving deep. "Let me hear you."

"Nearly," she breathed, trying to not fist her hand in his hair. "So good." Capturing her top lip in her teeth, she closed her eyes, focused on the sensation gathering low in her belly, chasing it, tightening around his fingers, her hand falling away to grasp the sheet.

"So good," she called again, encouraging him and suddenly she was filled, what had to be three fingers curving up inside her as he ground the heel of his palm into her clit. Full, so full, and that pressure edged the line of pleasure and pain, ripping her free from the moorings holding her back, letting her soar. She cried out when his teeth grazed her, nipping at the inside of her thigh, his weight and grip keeping her still as she climbed higher, thrown upwards to where the air was thin. Breath suspended, cocooned in the darkness behind her closed lids, ears deaf to anything except the rapid pounding of her heart.

"Jesus, honey," she heard him say from very nearby and realized his mouth was beside her head. Without her noticing, somehow in the past few moments he had moved up her body and was stretched over her. "You're fucking stunning."

Need. I need...

The feeling was overwhelming.

Please.

Never before had Mela felt so connected to a lover. Sex was about feeling good in the moment. Not this...*need*.

Hurley's hand bumped her belly, working between them and she lifted her hips, seeking. Then he was *there*, thrusting his cock deep with one long glide and holding, rotating his hips, grinding into her clit while his breath came fast and hard in her ear. Electric shocks rattled through her, centering between her legs as she stretched to accommodate him.

"Come again, honey, come on." He gritted the words out, forehead to an arm shoved in the mattress. "One more." Ass rolling, his thick cock plunging deeper, hips shifting side-to-side, then his hand was between them. "Come again." His thumb unerringly found her clit and pressed hard as his cock withdrew and then drove inside, hard and deep, slamming in and holding there as she rolled over that edge again. She lifted up to meet his movements, offering him everything, her head pushing backwards. The strain in his tone was gratifying when he grunted, "Fuck yeah, gorgeous, fuck me back."

Again taking the arch of her neck as an invitation, he trailed hard, hot kisses along the column of her throat, working her skin with teeth and tongue. On the sweet downward glide from the orgasm, her arms curved around his back to hold him tightly when with a ripple of power under her palms, he began to move with purpose. Muscled thighs working between her legs, he fucked her with passion and finesse. The air in the van became heated, close, sweat collecting on their skin until she felt his belly slipping and sliding across hers, his arms pressing into the mattress.

Shifting, he moved and found a different angle and approach that caused her to suck in a hard breath because it was *so* good. *Dios*. She drove up against him, tipping her hips, and he plunged deeper.

"Fuck, honey."

Fingers plucking at her nipples, Hurley's back bowed as one palm lifted a breast to his mouth. He sucked, drawing hard while his hand stroked across her skin. More sensation to overwhelm her, hard teeth and smooth lips nibbling along her jaw. It was as if he were everywhere at once, and she recognized that familiar tension low in her belly with some surprise. "Hurley," she breathed, bucking up against him again, driving him deeper, "nearly there."

"Fuck, honey, you comin' again?" There was an honest, pleased note of pride in his voice, and she laughed softly, pulling a gasp from him. "*God*. Do that again, gorgeous. Laugh for me." When she did, mouth to the skin of his shoulder, he groaned, the sound so ragged she realized he was losing grip on his control, hips plunging, now wildly chasing his own needs. The knowledge that she could bring this beautiful man here, give him this, draw this kind of passion from him was enough to drag her even closer.

Sounds of their bodies slapping together echoed and she heard the van's suspension creak and groan, mechanical singing nearly drowning out the noises flowing from her mouth. His mouth on her breast, teeth grazing across her nipple, hard cock deep inside her—everything conspiring to push her over and up and she was flying again. Muscles convulsing, she felt her body stiffen underneath his, anchoring herself with arms wrapped around his shoulders, tensing and clenching around him everywhere they touched.

Skin-covered muscles too addictive a draw, her mouth found the corded side of his neck, muffling her quiet cries and leaving a mark with a sucking kiss as he groaned, thrusting far inside her and holding there, his body bucking with release and pleasure. Pressing deep, and then withdrawing slightly before crashing into her again, hard and relentless. He ground out her name with a voice scraped raw, arms tightening around her as he came.

They rested like that for several minutes before moving. Then slowly, as if he were returning to life, Hurley's hands stroked down her sides, then up, and down again. Mela's arms curved around his back, palms pressed against his heated skin. Her thighs cradled his hips as their breath slowed and eased.

"Damn, baby." The muttered words were gentle, pleased, signaling satisfaction. He shifted away and as he pulled out she barely clamped her lips shut in time to stop the complaining noise she wanted to make. Wanted to give voice to the sorrow at losing the gratification of having him inside her, the intimate sense of connection she felt. A movement between them that she belatedly recognized as him ensuring a condom stayed in place. She realized she hadn't even worried about protection, hadn't asked him anything before opening her body to him. *Dios, soy loco*.

He stretched out beside her, hands gliding across her body for long minutes, each touch slow and lingering, relaxing her. Mapping her flesh with fingertips, she wanted the memory of his caress permanently impressed on her skin.

Hurley hummed deep in his chest, one hand curling around her waist as he tugged her closer. “You need to go to your tent, or can you stay with me?”

Shit.

That single question told her he was back in the prospect headspace. He would now be nervously considering the politics of what they had just done; no longer caught up in the moment of shared passion and craving. His question seemed to imply it would be better for her to disappear. Leave him to sleep and wake alone, granting him plausible deniability if there were harsh questions about fucking the Machos’ princess. *Always the same.* Everything was always about the club, which is why she never slept with members.

Fuck, she fumed. *What was I thinking?* Aloud, hiding the wound he’d opened with his rejection, she quietly said, “I never got my tent set up, but I can sleep in my bag, it’s no big deal.” Glad for the sheltering darkness, she tried to still her trembling lips as she sat up, groping for her clothing, looking for a way to escape gracefully.

His hands found hers, bringing her search to a halt as he said, “No, honey. Stop thinking so hard. I ain’t kicking you out. I want you to sleep here, with me, but I don’t want you to be embarrassed in the morning.” Lifting her gaze, she saw the shadows shift as he tilted his head, his hair falling to one side as he asked, “Sleep with me, honey?”

He twisted to lie down, and his hold on her hands pulled her with him, taking them both back down to the mattress. With a relieved sigh, she rested against his side. *He wants me to stay.* “Let me be your pillow,” he said, reaching to lift her head and slide his arm underneath it, pulling her tighter against him.

He gently pressed his lips to her hair, and whispered, "Sleep, gorgeous." She had arrived at the campsite already exhausted from both her cross-country ride and the tension of avoiding pursuit. With the encouragement of his sweeping caresses, those factors combined with the aftereffects of their shared passion conspired to pull her under the comforting blanket of oblivion quickly.

Hurley

Jesus. Hurley was stretched out on his back, staring into the darkness shrouding the van's ceiling. Resting against him was one of the prettiest girls he'd ever met. So gorgeous you'd expect the attitude she'd been throwing at him out by the bonfire. So beautiful you knew to the soles of your boots she wouldn't be worth it because she'd be busting your balls every single goddamned day, which would mean fucking her wouldn't be sweet. Fuck, no. A girl like that? Fucking would be revenge. Payback sex, and while he liked a good choke fuck, he wasn't into hating the bitch he was balling.

Mela was good at her game. So good, you might overlook the signs that she wasn't really the kind of bitch she liked to play. But he'd been looking, been watching. *Oh, yeah. Had my eyes on her*. Watching as closely as possible, studying her every move. Ever since she freaked out when he touched her. When her eyes went wide and blank, looking like a deer trapped in the flare of headlights, unsure which way to dart to avoid the danger barreling down on her. Hurley had retreated, fast, because he'd seen that look before. Ruby and Eddie, who belonged to Bear, had that look sometimes. So did Gunny's old lady, Sharon, and every Rebel knew her backstory.

Mela had come from New Mexico; he'd seen the plate on her bike.

New Mexico meant a lot of things. Duck, one of the brothers from Chicago, had been out there recently. Shit happened to the family of a club the Rebels were not just friendly with, but from what Hurley heard, considered as partners, the Southern Soldiers. Prospects were excluded from church, still, the news made the rounds, and everyone knew that Duck had rescued the daughter of the Soldiers' president from certain death, smack dab in the middle of a conflict with a Rebel enemy. *Diamante MC*. He sucked in a hard breath, listening as Mela's hair shifted, rustling quietly as her head lifted and fell with the movement of his chest.

Hurley had met that chick, knew Mela wasn't her, but the look in Bella's eyes was exactly like the burden Mela carried. Someone had hurt her like *that*, a scar that ran soul deep. His arm tightened, pulling her closer to his side. Her hand moved in response, sliding up his chest to rest directly above his heart. She sighed in her sleep, peaceful, relaxing against him.

So gorgeous. So damaged. *So needy*.

Damn, she ran hot. Hotter than anything he'd had before. Hot, tight, wet, and willing. *Fuck*. He scowled up at the ceiling, willing his dick back to sleep. He knew he wasn't shit in the sack, but he'd never felt that kind of closeness before. Never had been certain, without the woman directing him, what the bitch needed to find the "O" at least once. He'd never intentionally left a woman he fucked high and dry, but if she didn't get there and didn't let him know what revved her motor, he wouldn't go looking for the switch.

With Mela though, he'd been able to read her like a book. She let him explore every inch of her, felt good, tasted better, and fucked like an animal. From the stinging lines scored on his back, she'd liked what they'd done. Not afraid to show him, either. Gorgeous, inside and out, she hadn't been afraid of him, and he ate up the trust she gave him, pushing them both to the limit. Out by the bonfire, he'd discovered that she could be sweet, and was smart as hell. So fucking smart, he would never know why she took his hand, following him into the darkness. Glad she did, gratified she let him lead her back to this van. A place that had been purgatory before she'd entered. Now, heaven.

That's what he'd been thinking when he undressed her. An angel had come to rest in front of him. Beautiful, but didn't know it, and that shit wasn't an act. He'd been around bitches who pretended they didn't know what they looked like, falsetto voice as fake as their beauty in the end. Mela wasn't one of those. She'd trusted him again, sitting there on the cheap mattress looking like a princess. Like a Greek goddess come to life and she was about to let him touch her. Him, a prospect, but not in her eyes. He didn't have to earn a place beside her, she was willing to accept him as he was. Arms wide, ready to embrace what he could give her.

Angel. Goddess. *Queen*.

Mouth between her legs, he'd had to anchor her hips with one arm, holding her in place as he tongue- and finger-fucked her mindless. Never had he enjoyed the intimacy so much as with her. Never had he delved deep inside a woman, again and again, just to hear her cry out, to see how high he could bring her. When her fingers tugged his hair he'd nearly gone insane, mouth clamped hard around her, sucking deep—*he shifted, his balls pulling up tight at the memory*—until she came, body writhing. *I did that to her*, he thought, reaching down with the arm not curled around her, gripping his cock and squeezing hard.

He'd serve her every day if she let him. Take his time, learn what she wanted and liked, push hard until she came, shattering with his name in her mouth a million times. His bones sang with the truth that she was as in-tune with him as he was her, and knew instinctively what he needed. Made him feel like a goddamned king. *I'd give her the world if I could.*

He stretched and snuggled closer, nuzzling into her hair and wrapping her up in his arms as his eyes drifted closed. *Fucking gorgeous queen.*

Carmela

Disoriented, she startled awake, her heart pounding, and froze in place at the feeling of a large, hot, male body next to her. There was a sudden thrill of fear at the thick arms wrapped around her, one palm cupping her bare ass cheek. Then, as memories of where she was and who was next to her slowly slid into place, her heart rate slowly returned to normal. Hurley had wanted her here, had asked her to stay.

He was sleeping heavily, his breathing deep and even, relaxed and easy in his dreams. Mela reached out with one hand, using the pad of her thumb to trace his features, dragging his chin down, gently parting his lips. Barely breathing, she whispered her goodbye, "Was a good night, Hurley." Carefully extricating herself from his grip, dressing as quietly as possible, she eased the door of the van open. Once outside, she pulled it closed just as slowly and silently as she could, hearing it latch into place with an inevitability that was so poignant she had to blink away sudden tears.

Walking towards her bike, she pulled out her phone to see it was early morning, and from the blush of light in the sky, she knew the sun would be peeking over the horizon before long. With a sigh, she looked around and realized everyone else was still sleeping, except for a lone figure seated near the remains of the bonfire. Moving that direction, she recognized DeeDee, resting comfortably in a chair with a quilt drawn around her shoulders, staring at the glowing embers of the banked fire.

Silently Mela sat down on the grass beside her, eyes already fixed on the flickering cinders.

DeeDee hummed, then asked, "What's up, buttercup?" From the corner of her eye, she saw her friend turn to glance Mela's way before facing the fire again. "There's just something about a fire. It's mesmerizing when at this stage. The early blaze is full of energy and heat, wild and chaotic. Out of control. But, if you let things go far enough, you wind up with this calmness. It's still hot as hell, just more stable, less riotous. You know the fire burning down to coals like this means it's nearing the end of its life, but it's still so beautiful."

She leaned against DeeDee's legs and sighed. Without looking away from the flames, Mela said, "Daddy didn't want me to come."

"We know, sweetheart. Estavez called Slate and Mason straight away when you left. He told them you were on your way, and he'd have men on you the whole trip." DeeDee offered this knowledge without hesitating.

"I'd have been here earlier yesterday, but I ditched them. I didn't tell Daddy where we were planning to camp, so I thought I could escape the scrutiny for at least a couple of days," she said and sighed again. "Slate probably told Daddy exactly where this place is already, so that was useless. Wasted effort. They'll come roaring in here soon, all pissed off because they got played, and they're gonna make me leave."

"No, they won't." DeeDee's voice was clear and firm. "Your father would have preferred that scenario, but Slate talked him down. Told him he'd have his best men in place to keep us all safe." She pointed towards the van. "Hurley here with us, and three men staged along the road. You rode past them to get in, and if it anyone other than you had approached, that person would have never made it a hundred feet up the road."

"I just get so tired of everything," Mela muttered, propping her head in her hand. "It's always about the club. Real shit. Made up shit. Doesn't matter. I can't do anything just for me."

"We should have made Eddie come, babies or not," DeeDee said with a soft laugh, referencing another of the Rebel women, one whose father had also been a club president. "Growing up as she did, she could relate, for sure. But Carmela," her tone became serious, "you more than most know what happened to Watcher's daughter at the hands of their enemies. That's not made up. You saw her, helped care for her. You know he's lucky Bella lived, honey, and she's never going to be the same. You can't be angry with your father for fearing it could happen to you. There is unrest in the clubs" —Mela raised her head to retort, but DeeDee pushed on— "I know what you're going to say, and I've used the same argument sweetheart, because there is *always* unrest, but this is a level we've not seen in decades. Something is building, and our men don't yet have a handle on exactly what. So, when something like that happens to a powerful man's family, a president's daughter, all the men in our lives pay attention. Like it or not, you are your father's daughter, which means you are a target."

Hurley

He had woken abruptly, every sense singing danger, screaming at him that something had changed. In those first few moments of awareness his gut had filled with a rolling sense of unease. As he scanned the inside of the van, there was nothing overtly out of place, everything looked as he expected, but hadn't been able to shake the feeling that something important was missing.

It had taken him two carefully metered breaths to realize the body that had been so sweetly curled into him, the heat and presence he'd enjoyed lying beside was gone. *Dammit, she ran after all.* She'd surrendered to her own wants, and fuck, but he was glad she did. *Fucking amazing lay*. Smart and funny, she'd certainly raised the bar for chicks in his bed. Mela had been so hesitant from the beginning, seemingly fearful until she let go her control and gave herself to him. That fear creeping back in nearly immediately, but she'd stayed. *Amazing woman*. Gone.

I asked her to stay. Hurley'd asked, and she'd given in, burrowing into him as if she couldn't get close enough. Stretched out beside him, hand on his chest. Head pillowed on his shoulder, the scent of her had surrounded him. He'd watched her sleeping, smiling at the little snuffling noises she made, liking how she snuggled into his side, trusting even at rest.

Turning things over in his mind, he'd found he wanted...no, *needed* to know more about her. She wasn't an old lady, nor a fender bunny. A puzzle to solve. She was here at the chick campout, which meant she was well known to the

Rebels or she wouldn't have been trusted with the location of this little party, but he didn't know her from Adam. *Or Eve*.

So beautiful, her face and body were spectacular, unforgettable, but he'd never laid eyes on her before. A temptation from the beginning, opening his eyes to find her looking him over had been a thrill. Naked and rousing to hard within a moment, it hadn't been easy tamping down his desires. His mouth watered at the thought of her and breathing deep, he caught a trace of her scent on the air. *I'll for-fucking-sure remember that woman*.

Dressing quickly, he exited the van, taking care to close the door quietly. Two figures were seated near the bonfire from last night, Mela and DeeDee. Even from here he could see he was right, Mela had leaned into the older woman. They were friends, wind sisters, if not club.

Moving close enough to eavesdrop, DeeDee's words hit him like a blow. *She's a fucking princess*. Someone precious to his president. Important to his brothers, and like he thought last night, far out of his reach. *Not my queen*. Then the rest of what DeeDee said sank in, and he realized that this assignment was critical, like she'd tried to tell him before. Not a punishment detail, but an honor. He shifted his shoulders, feeling the leather slide across his bare skin. Something asked of every brother, part of the written bylaws, to protect the things each man held most dear. Club, brothers, family.

Now there were things he needed to know to plot his path. One, he needed to know Mela's connections so he could understand. Two, DeeDee had to give him a sign that what he'd done wasn't going to fuck things up. All the women would follow her lead, even Ruby eventually, so if she were in favor of his liaison with Mela, then he wouldn't have to fight as hard to keep her.

Keep her?

She sat facing the fire, dim flickering glow from the flames glancing across her skin, hair gathered over one shoulder. Gorgeous. Not happy with her lot in life, either, it seemed. *I could make her happy. I did last night*. Not just the sex, either. The talking before, the way she looked at him when he complimented her. Her easy laughter at his stories. The way she'd leaned in to kiss him. *I could mean something to her*.

Keep her? *Oh, hell yeah.*

Carmela

"What kind of target?" Hurley's voice came from right behind DeeDee, and Mela jumped, twisting around. "And who is your father?" She stared at him for a minute, finding he looked different in the light cast from the fire's coals. His hair a dull red and the expression on his face angry, striped with lines of shadow and fury.

Without responding, she stood and walked to her bike, lifted her jacket from the handlebars and unfolded it, turning so the weak light from the fire illuminated the patches on the back. Hurley's eyes went wide as he read the club's information, and her title, and he said, "No shit?"

DeeDee answered him with a soft laugh. "Shit-free, totally."

"So we got the national president's cousin who's also a leverage member's old lady, my chapter president's old lady, a member's old lady, and now another club's national president's fucking daughter? Goddamned Machos?" He held up four fingers, "DeeDee, Ruby, Kathy...and Mela?"

DeeDee nodded, twisting in her chair to face him. "And four of their best friends, who also have a place in your national president's heart." She paused, staring up at him. "It's a stern charge, Hurley. Slate believed you up for the job, but you have only to make a single call to pull in others. Your decision," she said and turned back so she could watch the fire again. He didn't respond other than with a nod that DeeDee didn't see, and then turned and silently stalked past Mela, moving back towards the van.

Gaze to the ground, she slowly refolded her jacket, again draping it over the handlebars of her bike. Her chest was tight with the pain and shame of a rejection she had expected, but it hurt no less for that. She thought to herself, *Well, that is that, and if you thought it could ever be more than that, you were loco, chica.*

Princess status in her father's club meant few men were brave enough to even befriend her, and none had ever wanted her enough to dare wade through the politics and pressure of a relationship. Today looked to be no different.

A touch on her arm interrupted her thoughts, and she looked up, stunned to see Hurley standing there, his palm sliding down the inside of her wrist, fingers threading through hers. "Come back to bed, honey," he said, leaning in for a kiss. Then, tugging at their joined hands, he led her back to the van, claiming her, even if their audience was limited to one broadly grinning and overly protective mother figure.

Slate

"Fuck me," Slate muttered, rolling his eyes at Ruby. She was standing in the kitchen bottle-feeding Kayley, one of their infants, while their two oldest stood, each holding tight to a leg of Ruby's jeans. Allen and Dani were babbling incessantly back and forth, by turns grinning and frowning. Their oldest set of twins had been actively building a private language of late, which DeeDee assured him was normal. Privately, he thought it meant he and Ruby would be fucked at some point. Those two were already getting into everything. He expected that once they could scheme and plot together, their lives would be pure chaos.

Slate was cradling Hayley, twin sister to the one in Ruby's arms, tipping a bottle to her hungry mouth to quiet her vocal complaints. "You're serious? Mela hooked up with Hurley?"

Grinning widely, Ruby nodded. Leaning down to nuzzle Kayley's cheek, she told him, "Humping like bunnies in the van." She giggled. "He was really sweet with her, you shoulda seen it. I kinda like him for her. It's a good match."

Allen plopped down to the floor, then rocked over so he could crawl away, his ass comically swaying side-to-side as he moved out of sight through the arch that led to the living room. Dani watched him go for a moment, then tipped her head back, eyes far more calculating than Slate liked flicking over him before latching onto her mother's face. The babble from before changed, and he grinned to hear her calling, "Da. Da. Dadada. *DA!*" while looking up at Ruby. Distracted, he was startled when a crash came from the living room, toenails clicking a mad retreat on the hardwood floor as the beagle they were dog-sitting tried to escape the boy. That was followed by squeals of laughter from Allen.

"You don't fuckin' like Hurley, Ruby. Why would you want him for my Mela?" Hayley had lost the nipple, and her tiny fists flailed for a moment, then she quietened when he teased her bottom lip with it, her chin bobbing as she sought it again. "She deserves—"

"A man who makes her feel safe. A man who would turn the world upside down to make her happy." She gave him one of those smiles, the ones that nearly took his knees out from underneath him. The smiles that he worked every day to earn. Even now, almost four years into the relationship with her, she could floor him with a single look. Her voice was soft when she continued, "A man like you."

"Fuck me."

End

MASON'S MUSINGS #3

MARIALISA DEMORA

Facebook Group
Blog entry

My Boy

This blog entry by Mason falls after Duck, book #8 in the RWMC series.

Mason

Mornin'. Hope you're off to a fine start to your day.

One of the things the Boss Lady tells me all the time is to just be myself when I'm feelin' chatty. Woman's a little cracked, if you ask me. Who the hell else would I be if not just me?

I know a bunch of you have some idea of my journey through life on this old earth ball, but I'd be surprised if there weren't areas that were still gray. Here be dragons territory, if you will.

Some stories are too hard to recount. At least in the moment, when they're fresh, you know? Get a little time between the then and now, and it's less acute.

I missed out on so much with Chase. Born to a bitch who held news of his paternity back, and I'll never understand that. Struggling for money like she was, you'd have thought Carrie would have leveraged the boy differently. She didn't, and he wasn't much of a kid anymore by the time Watcher found him for me. Bitch had torn that away from him in huge bleeding chunks, making him live alongside her like she did.

So in a way Willa's given me another chance with Garrett and Dolly. God, watching her body change as she carried our babies was life changing. Knowing she had my future in her belly, our future--damn, I get overcome just thinkin' about it.

Holding her, being there when she brought our babies to air, that's a blessing and an honor I will never take for granted.

Hard to reconcile the man inside me who can love Willa so much, and fuckin' hate Carrie like I do. If she wasn't already dead, I'd fuckin' kill her for what she did to Chase. When they opened the cell where her body was, I didn't feel an ounce of remorse for feelin' the way I did. The way I do.

Still, she was my boy's mother.

A couple of years ago he asked if we could take a trip to Kentucky and all it took was a look at the calendar to know what was up. Her birthday, and I figured Chase was feelin' nostalgic, missin' his mom, even if she was a shitty one.

I couldn't have been more wrong.

Oh, he wanted to go to the grave, but it wasn't for the reasons I thought.

We got there and I stood a little away, not wanting to crowd the boy. Give him some space to do whatever he needed, say his goodbyes or whatever. This was the first time we'd been to the cemetery, and his first time to see the stone planted at the head of her grave.

It just took a minute for me to realize I was wrong, that my boy needed me close, his clenched fists gave away what his shaking shoulders tried to hide, so I wrapped an arm around his neck and pulled him close, lending him my strength. Long as he needed it, I'd be there.

You wanna know what his reason was for goin'? Boy was leading up to something, that's for sure.

"I'm glad it's just her name." That's what he told me.

"What other name would be on there?" You can understand why I was puzzled, yeah?

"I didn't want it to say 'mother of' or anything." He turned away from the grave then, and I let him walk away a couple of steps. "I didn't want my name there."

"Why not, Chase?"

"She was never my mother. Not really." I just let the silence hang between us, because I knew he wasn't done talking yet. "Willa's more a mother than Carrie ever was." I'd forgotten his egg donor wanted him to call her by her name, not Mom. "You think...you think Willa'd want me? Legal like?"

It hit me then, just how much weight Chase had carried for way too long. Here he was, only a couple years away from being an adult in his own right, and asking for a woman we both loved to be his mother.

"I think she'd be tickled if you wanted that, Chase. Tickled, and pleased." I put a hand on the back of his neck and squeezed. "We'll get shit started Monday."

I was right about how Willa reacted. She was pregnant with Gar-boy, but you'd have never known it from her jumpin' around.

Chase looked at me over her shoulder, submitting to yet another hug and the smile in his eyes was everything I wanted to see.

My boy's a lot like me. He lives life to the fullest, loves deep, and trust comes hard to him. He's a good boy. He'll find his way.

RAY NELMS: A STUDY IN INSANITY

MARIALISA DEMORA

DEDICATION

Because we don't get to pick our family, this is dedicated to mine. You got lucky.

ACKNOWLEDGMENTS

For a long time I've wondered about the bad guys in my stories. How did they turn out the way they are? Was it nature, bred deep in their bones? Or could it be strictly nurture, stained into their souls from the time they stood at the knees of those who raised them? Could their paths have been altered, given the right push at the right time?

Age old questions, right? Still. I wonder.

Ray Nelms is one of my bad guys who just won't be quiet. Even in Duck's story, he seemed to long to have his fifteen minutes of fame, breaking through and into Duck's dreams. And because I wonder … now here he is, given center stage in his own story.

Is the attention deserved? Well, I guess you'll have to be the judge of that, won't you? Let me know if you get a minute, would ya?

Woofully yours,
~ML

Chapter One

This first-time-published short story falls after Duck in the timeline of the series. Welcome to Ray's mind, it's an uncomfortable place to be.

RAY

Staring at the shadows traveling at a predictable pace across the ceiling, Ray Nelms felt at peace. As the van's suspension bounced and swayed, he went with the motion, and rolled gently side to side like waves crawling up the seashore. *Glad Reuben wasn't there*. The disappointment on his big brother's face would have killed him, and even now, seeing it only through his imagination, Ray's stomach ached.

There was freedom in knowing the pain he'd carried for so long was about to end.

Now that he was no longer in the grip of frenzied need that had come over him on the county fairgrounds, it was so clear where everything had gone all wrong. Not just for tonight, but perhaps even throughout his life.

He suspected if he'd ever been to see a shrink, they would have done a better job pinpointing where things had gone off the rails. *Woulda had a field day shrinking me*. Where nature met nurture in such a way that it threw his life askew. He knew all the words, knew the diagnoses and labels that would likely have been applied to him as a kid. Doing the things he'd done, seeing what he'd seen—a shrink would have been sympathetic, no doubt. Even as the signed the orders locking him away.

"Not his fault," he wheezed out, pitching his voice two octaves higher than normal. He bit down on his tongue before his traitorous mouth could respond to the ghost voices in his head, tasting bright copper as his teeth tore the flesh.

I wonder if this is how Daddy felt. His fingers twitched involuntarily as if they were once again wrapped around that age-wizened throat. His old man hadn't fought it. *Knew it was time, I guess*. At the end, he'd lifted one ice-cold hand, curling around Ray's wrist, the pressure of that grip so weak it was laughable. *The only way to curb the man was to kill him*. The old man had taken to going to Mexico, down past the bridge and into the warren of streets that could lead to paradise or hell, depending on your poison. *One of those times I tried so hard to stuff it in a box*, he remembered. The sickness that lived inside him eating at him for weeks and months at a time, before he knew that denying the need only made it grow stronger. Just the smell following his father home after a trip down to Mexico had been enough to wake the beast within Ray. Sex, depravity, blood, and terror. *Had to kill him*.

A man seated nearby turned to stare out the van's back doors. He announced, "We're clear," as if everyone would understand what that meant.

Someone in the front of the van responded, "Two more fences. Wanna get well away from the roads."

Smart. Ray was glad he was being bested by someone who knew their shit when it came to disposing bodies. *I could still probably teach 'em a thing or two.* He snorted, taking care to keep it quiet.

How many have I killed? Closing his eyes to focus, he quickly lost himself amid details of favorite scenes. Imagery burned into his brain, not only from each event but from studying photographs he'd taken. Trophies he'd kept safe, only bringing the images out when the need was on him, hoping the evidence of his handiwork would keep those twisted desires at arm's length. Trying to hold off as long as he could.

The brunette struggled, her wiry strength a surprise, making it an exciting challenge. She'd come willingly to Ray's trailer, and given her body over to him in a show of trust. As a gift, he'd gotten her off, working her with skill until she cried out, overwhelmed by the sensations. A stand-in for Mica, her face was red in the heated air of the trailer, framed by black locks. Shadows from the uncertain lighting making her cheekbones look even more prominent, the First Nation blood rearing its head.

He didn't intend to kill her. Not yet. After planning his game for weeks, following her around the circuit, learning everything he could about her, there was no way he wanted to cut his fun short. Sure, his work meant he'd learned what she liked, but even more critical to his plan, he'd taken care to learn her fears.

Everyone had a fear that could cripple. Everything, *he corrected himself. Ray casually adjusted his hold on her, the blood that kept her alive coursing millimeters underneath his hand. "You're afraid," he murmured, watching red bloom in one eye, staining the sclera in an uneven oval. "Afraid of losing."*

That had been the goad to get her to this event, telling her the biggest names would pass the show by, leaving points for the picking. "Wasn't wrong. Didn't lie." She stopped moving, and he relaxed his grip, rewarded when her body pulled in a breath so deep her back arched.

Thumb to her carotid, he waited, feeling her pulse even out slowly but surely. When her eyes opened and landed on him, that oh-so gentle thrum raced again. "Afraid of losing, and now—" He tightened his grip, pushing his thumb deeper into her flesh, satisfied with how it gave under the power of his hand. "—me."

The selected location had been critical, because those particular fairgrounds butted up against a pork operation, double layers of confinement hogs waiting out their lives with restricted movement, carefully monitored diets, and artificially constructed days.

Everything worked out as he'd planned, almost. *Still, I learned something for the future,* he reminded himself. Circling through the town weeks later he'd picked up a copy of the local newspaper to see the missing woman had been found. Well, parts of her. Seemed pigs didn't digest teeth. *Always willin' to add to my bank of knowledge*.

Hogtied ankles to wrists, Ray was trussed up like a missionary on a cannibal's spit. *Not my kink*. The thought stirred another memory, curdled in a far corner of his brain.

For a time, he had partnered with a man who got off on biting women they shared. Latching tight, he would suck hard, coming up for air with blood on his teeth and gums, lips painted red. Ray had missed the work done alongside his father—an image of Reuben flashed through his head—*their* father. Had hoped the man would fill that singing need.

The man didn't. He couldn't. In the end, he'd been just another disposal site marked on a map shoved in a drawer in the trailer.

Wonder what they'll make of my stuff? Ray kept the sensitive tools in his climate-controlled trailer, those expensive and specialized toys needing particular care to remain effective. Researched at anonymous computer kiosks, then purchased in well-trafficked, out of the way places, his face forgettable unless he wanted to be remembered. White hat through and through when he was on supply runs like that.

Of the common tools—these not being ones for rodeo or even construction, but for slaughterhouses—most were tucked into a container deep in the toolbox of his truck. Chemicals stored in plain sight, placed inside the feed bin alongside tubs of vitamins for the horses he occasionally hauled for pay. As a bull rider, he didn't need to transport his own livestock, but he liked the freedom having a mobile base of operations gave him.

At three dozen murders, Ray gave up counting, abandoning his obscene cataloging. Instead, he turned his mind back to the beginning, those frustrating failures.

The ones like Mica Scott. Like Molly Scott. Like Anabelle Taylor, Lisa Kennwort, and Tiffany Wabash.

The ones who got away.

The familiar curl of fear crawled up his spine, wrapping around so it settled in his belly. Failure wasn't allowed. Failure meant there was someone in the world who knew secrets about him, something he'd been schooled from twelve to never allow.

On nights when their father had a visitor in his shed, the hallway stretching the length of the house felt twice as long. Ray dragged each step, holding to every slow second before he had to face the window in his room. Thin glass, it did nothing to hold back sounds emanating from the shed in the backyard, that twelve-foot-square section of hell. Tonight, it held a sweet waitress from town, smile plastered on her face as she climbed out of the ranch truck, her fancy dress telling a tale of desire. Ray attended school with her daughter. He wouldn't be able to look the girl in the face tomorrow.

Reuben's door opened as Ray attempted to sneak past. "He got someone?" Only a year separated them, and the boys protected each other as best they could. Ray nodded. Reuben studied him for a minute, then asked, "It gonna get bad?" Ray swallowed and nodded again. Reuben whirled and slugged the wall, puffs of plaster evidence of a hit hard enough to crack the drywall. "Why does he have to be like this?" Turning back, Reuben stared at him for a minute. "Someone's got to stop him. One of these times he's going to really hurt someone. Hurt 'em bad."

Ray saw the courage his brother pulled together and knew he couldn't allow what Reuben was about to do. The way their father felt about Reuben, an unreasonable hatred of his firstborn son, Ray's brother going out and interrupting things would mean more than a beating for him. It could mean…anything. Once their father was in the grip of his compulsion, being in his way was one of the most dangerous places to be. Their ranch foreman had done that last year, pounding on the shed's door, shouting for Nelms to stop.

It had been the foreman's daughter that time, making the man's urgency understandable as he tried to stop the train wreck from happening. Instead, it had been a wreck of a different kind, and through the thin glass, Ray had seen their father load a tarp-covered bundle in the back of the truck. Ray followed him to the gully where they dumped dead cows refused by the renderer, then watched as the foreman's limp body tumbled to the bottom. A cascade of rotting carcasses followed him down, covering the corpse in moments.

All for nothing.

One night later the girl was back in the shed, her screams finding no hero that time.

"I'll go," Ray said suddenly, not knowing where the words came from. "He doesn't hate me as much."

"No," Reuben argued. "You don't need to see that."

Ray laughed.

Six hours later he stumbled back upstairs. His hair, clothes...hell, his skin smelled of smokes, booze, and sex. Reuben was waiting and the moment he saw Ray, it was like a door closed in his face. From that night on, Reuben hated him.

Was that the beginning? He wondered as the van rolled across another cattle guard.

It was heady at first. Ray liked the rush of commanding another being and having them do his bidding. His father treated him as a collaborator, someone he could bounce ideas off. One night, well into his whiskey, his father shared that hearing what they would be doing seemed to ratchet up the tension for their partners. Only much later did Ray realize those first months were tame compared to what their father was used to doing. *Easing me into the role I cast for myself.*

In his head, he had always excused their actions because, as his father had said time and again, the women came to them. Consensual, agreed upon encounters, they were looking for safe kink far different from what their husbands found down in Mexico. In his head, Ray had believed all of that meant it was normal. Edging closer and closer to the black boundaries, still, *they got what they asked for*. Twelve-year-old Ray had held to that.

The first time the old man killed a partner it came as a shock. Large, calloused hands wrapped around the woman's neck until her face purpled, the color matching her bound breasts. She had thrashed as much as the bindings allowed, and still, his father didn't release his hold. Ray had watched her go limp, and thinking she'd passed out, had joined his father in jacking off on her immobile body. Only afterward did he realize what had happened.

I didn't sleep for a week, he remembered, pressing his lips together. *Such a newbie.*

Delirious with fatigue, Ray had burned the shed in a fit of remorse. Their father had blamed Reuben, beaten him within an inch of his life. *Didn't change a thing, except the location of the playtimes.*

Now, understanding too well the work that went into building something like their father had in the shed, Ray knew his father's reaction was mild. *It was me, I woulda killed Rue.*

The murder had been the turning point for everything, an act that bound him so tightly to their father, Ray knew he'd never get free. *Rue could, though. Made sure 'o that.* Each night building on previous ones, serving to open that gaping dark inside him wider. *Been filled with poison so long, don't know what it'd feel like to be clean.*

Lessa. His wife had been clean, through and through. *Loved her, much as I was able.* When Ray married Lessa, the easy availability of sex had relieved a portion of the strain inside him. Lessa's sweet nature eased it even more.

He'd picked her out of a bar full of pretty women not for her beauty, but because she looked so much like...*Mica*. The bitch who was the reason behind him being on the floor of this van right now. *Goddamned Mica.*

Lessa thought she could fix him. Believed if she were sweet, pleased him in bed, cleaned his house, or was enough of anything...he'd change. *Wrong*. His lips split when they drew back across his teeth in a savage smile. Every attempt she made only enraged him because it'd rile up his father. Get the old man talking about what he'd like to do to sweet Lessa. *Couldn't stand to think of his hands on her. She was mine*. Ray had run those months through his head repeatedly over the years, never finding a different outcome. *Once Daddy got involved, it was inevitable.*

The coroner stalked up the basement hallway in the hospital, face angry. He didn't know what his father had over the man, since more than one death got covered up over the years. Every time, the man swore it was the last. But then Ray's father would make a call, and the man would pick up. Now, however, the coroner looked outraged.

Closer, the man reached up and slapped Ray in the chest with papers clutched in his hand, held them there and pushed hard, forcing Ray back one step, then a second, before the wall caught him, holding him firm. A moment passed, then the man ground out words that echoed in Ray's head, tossing his stomach up into his throat for a moment. "She was pregnant."

That can't be right. *He and Lessa talked about kids, sure, but in a far future sort of way. A one day way, when life would be normal and he'd feel right about bringing another being into the world. Once the sickness inside him crawled into a box and stayed there for longer than a minute. Once Lessa fixed him. "What?" His throat closed over the question so it came out in a croak, sounding like the trafficker he'd found deep in the desert, leading underage charges towards a fresh hell. Ray'd buried his knife under the man's chin, tongue pinned to the roof of his mouth, garbling his shouts and screams. "What do you mean?"*

"Means you get pinned for this, boy, it's a double homicide."

"She can't be." Hot and heavy, the tears threatened, clogging Ray's chest. "Not Lessa."

"She went easy," the man said, uncaring of the confusion Ray struggled through. "At least you gave her that."

"Better than letting my old man at her," Ray muttered his justification, the knowledge she was carrying his child loosening his mouth. "Better dead than that. You sure she was pregnant?"

"Yeah, about four months along."

Four months. *That would have put it about the time of Ray's father's last trip to Mexico. When Ray and she had the house to themselves for a week, and she'd loved him in a way that eased the strain. He always had seen it like a pustule inside him, growing larger and larger, the infection building every day until something happened to lance it off.* Rue's not this way, *he thought.* Just me. *"You know someone who does vasectomies?"*

The man's head jerked back and he stepped away, taking the rustling papers with him. "Yeah. Why?"

"Kill the bloodline with me."

The van jolted, and he twisted his neck, rocking with the movement as he stared up at the man seated closest. Ray watched him look out the front windows, then turn to glare out the back before declaring, "Good a place as any." The man bent close, and Ray felt the tension ease in his arms as the rope was removed from his ankles.

And thus is decided my place of death.

"How you wanna do this?" The driver's question was barely audible over the sounds in the van. "We need to send them something afterwards."

"You know how hard it is to get something out of your head?" Ray's elbow caught on something as they grabbed his boots and dragged him out. Arms over his head, the fabric of his rodeo competition shirt captured his attention for a moment. Sponsor patches competed for space, each of them hard won, sewn in place knowing the blood and sweat that went into a successful eight-second ride. "Like when you go off a bull the wrong way, you get hung up. Always seems like it takes a thousand years to loosen your knot, every jump yankin' your shoulder out of joint, fingers crushed in your glove, bull hatin' you because he can't get away from you. Over and over, and you can't get away. That's how it is. It gets locked into place and nothing can dislodge it. Hung up, hard. A lifetime."

His head impacted the van's bumper on the way down, breath knocking from his body as he hit the ground. Each gasp sucked in abrasive sand, causing a cascade of coughs. His voice croaked when he told them, "Mica was the key. When I had her, nothing could hold me back. Nothing could keep me down."

"Shut him up," the driver's voice complained, and the man who had sat over him on the funeral ride leaned close, yanked off the shades and stared intently. Ray stared back, seeing only hard-edged anger in the man's eyes.

Pulling back and tucking an arm of the glasses into the neck of his shirt, the man muttered, "His jawin' don't bother me none."

Ray needed to purge this bubble of guilt inside him before they ended him. "She was my sanity. I needed her so I could stay sane. I tried with so many others, but they never did it for me like she did. She was like a box I could stuff that sick shit in, and she'd lock it up tight. Keep it locked up for a long time." Sticks and dirt shoved under his vest and shirt as the men hauled him along the ground.

"Gotta take the vest off, it's got that shit bull riders wear."

"She went away." Ray tipped his head back, uncaring of the rocks and stones his skull hit and stared up into the man's face. "So many others. I couldn't find what I needed. I looked, man. *You gotta know I looked*. Never found another box like her. She's something special. Fixed the monster in me, the monster my old man made me into."

He twisted to see they were nearing a gully. A rabbit broke cover and streaked away out of sight. *Run, bunny. Run away*. "You got no idea how it feels to live with this inside me. It's always hated me, couldn't get away from me any more than I could escape it." The dragging stopped. "When the hell you live in is inside you, what do you do?"

A hand wrenched at his vest and he heard snaps and stitching give way. Struck by a sudden jolt of fear, he blurted something that often woke him up at night. "The families.

They'll never know." Arching his neck, he glared up. "They gotta know."

"On three." That was the driver's voice again, and Ray watched as the man standing in front of him reached to his back and brought out a gun. "One."

"Gotta know what, asshole?" Leveling the weapon, his expression was impassive.

"Two."

Ray looked into the darkness of the barrel and took a breath.

"Where they're buried."

Three.

Chapter Two

Graeme

Graeme stared down at the man lying in the dirt, three lethal bullet holes in his head and body, blood and fluids leaking out into the sand of the desert. "Did you hear what he said?"

Turk bent over, grabbing one of the dead man's arms. "Help me get him over there. Wind'll cover him with shit pretty fast if he's down in that little gully." When Graeme didn't move, Turk angled his head to stare up at him. "Jesus, Horse, fuckin' pull your weight here. I ain't doing this shit by myself."

Graeme suppressed the snarl that always tried to escape when someone called him that name. *I'm not that man anymore.* He hated it, a steady and painful reminder of his own past. Horse should have been abandoned when he left the last club, but sometimes things carried on, regardless of a man's damn wishes. *"When the hell you live in is inside you, what do you do?"* The bull rider's voice echoed through his head and he shoved that down, too. Stooping, he gripped a limp wrist and tugged, surprised as always at how heavy the dead could be. Together he and Turk wrangled the body to the nearby dip, letting it stay as it had landed, elbow angled up towards the sky, a wing that would never take flight.

A sand-filled gust of wind deposited the first wave of debris along the side of the corpse and Graeme kicked more on top of it, suddenly not wanting to see the man's slack face anymore. The corpse's eyes were still open and he felt as if everything they did was on display.

"Hold on, lemme get a pic. Blackie said they'd want one." Turk bent at the waist to angle his phone as he took several pictures, consulting the screen with each one, ensuring they met whatever standard was in his head.

"Did you hear him?" Graeme couldn't let it rest. "He said some of his kills were still out there."

"So?" Turk slammed the back doors of the van, then he and Graeme climbed into the vehicle. Twisting the key in the ignition, he asked, "You care?"

"If it were your sister, wouldn't you?"

Graeme could hear the sand crunching under their wheels and he angled his eyes to the side, watching the angular form of the body as it disappeared into the distance.

This wasn't the first cleanup and disposal he'd done since joining the Freed Riders. Blackie, their president, kept to most of the old school rules, and that was just fine with Graeme. He liked how things were predictable in the club. Had always liked when events in life followed a path he could track. Liked it better when men did the same.

And that was his problem with how things had shaken out today. Three of them, him, Turk, and a big man called Angry Mike, had picked up the bull rider outside Houston, and after their last similar run, it should have been Angry Mike's turn to ride with Turk. The two of them had a conversation while Graeme was in the bathroom at a truckstop, and before he knew it they were dropping Angry Mike off at a well-known whorehouse. Turk's laughing promise to pick him up on the way back had pissed Graeme off.

"You don't want to know what he meant? It doesn't pique your interest at all?" Graeme changed position, lifted a foot to the dash and wedged himself into the seat.

"Nope." Turk twisted a dial on the radio and the local DJ's voice swelled in volume, this a clear tactic to get Graeme to shut up about the dead guy.

~

MASON'S MUSINGS #4

MARIALISA DEMORA

Facebook Group
Blog entry

Quiet Start to My Day

This blog entry by Mason falls after Fury, story #11 in the RWMC series.

Mason

Mornin'. Boss lady's gonna be annoyed with me. Do I look like I give a fuck? She said Thursday, I heard Wednesday, so here I am. She'd prolly say I'm bein' chatty, and I guess in a way she's right. Just had some thoughts this mornin' and decided it might be good to get 'em down somehow.

It was quiet here this morning, house creaking, making soft sounds like it was breathing slowly, in and out. I sat on the back porch with my coffee, staring out at the horizon watching the sky gradually change from that deep indigo of night's last gasp into the sweet rose of sunrise.

Wasn't long before I heard it. The beautiful patter of little feet running through the house. Dolly, on her way to me, wanting a lil bit of daddy time. She's not quite strong enough to open the sliding glass door, so I cranked around in the patio chair--one my Willa had to have because it matched some flowerpot or something. *Jesus*. Don't tell her it's comfortable, or I'll never hear the end of it--and grabbed the handle just in time to clear the way for my baby girl to barrel through at full speed.

That's the way my Dolly lives, her and Garrett both. Full steam ahead, take no prisoners. I can already tell she and Gar-boy are going to be handfuls, probably a lot like their older brother Chase.

Chase. He's my puzzle-boy, my troubled kiddo, and there's no reason given to expect he wouldn't be, given the shit his egg donor put him through when he was little. Pisses me right the fuck off, because I've heard stories about shit that happened before I found him. Well, Watcher found him. Found him and brought me to him, giving me the greatest gift he ever could have. I have faith in my boy, though. He'll sort his ass out and decide what he needs soon enough. Love that kid.

Arms stretching up, no words needed, Dolly demanded to be lifted. I do as I'm told with this one, otherwise she'll wake the whole house. Got a set of lungs on her, and my girl ain't afraid to use them. She'd brought her blankie with her, and I was careful to tuck it around her little legs, bringing the tail of it up beside her head. She was waitin' for that, wrapped her little fingers around it and lay her head on my chest, pretty as you please, thumb between her lips as her eyes closed.

We stayed like that a while, my girl and me. A quiet start to a good day.

EXTRAS

MARIALISA DEMORA & FRIENDS

A Reader's Letter to Mason

Dear Mason,

I fell in love with you while you fell in love with Mica and as you let her go. Since then I have fallen harder for you as you mentor your brave and wonderful Rebels as they grow and find women of their own and I fell much more when you found your soulmate, Willa.

I never thought I could love someone as deeply as I did you and have kept you in the deepest part of my heart. You are such an amazing man and a wonder RWMC leader.

It breaks my heart to say...I have fallen for another. It is with my deepest and sincerest regret that I must tell you – with tears in my eyes – that Bones has won my heart.

With his use of words, so few yet poetic, Bones easily won my heart. He is such a good man (just as you are) and has a kind heart hidden under all his ink. And the way he views life and how he is with his Ester... I can't help but give him my heart in its entirety. I can't help but feel wonder when he speaks as he supports his friends and the advice he gives. I couldn't help but fall quickly, fall deeply and fall madly in love with a man named Bones.

I hope you will understand and forgive me. Please know that this was not a decision I made lightly and in all honesty it wasn't something I could have prevented. The heart wants what the heart wants, right? Please know that no matter what, you will always have a piece of me. But alas, my heart belongs to another.

With love—but no regrets—your admirer and fan,

Marie

A Reader's Prayer for Faynez

Dear Heavenly Saint Savio, Saint Christopher and Saint Valentine, please guide Momma Rebel in her time of need and help her to figure out how to get Faynez out of this predicament. Help Momma Rebel provide the written guidance that she needs. Take this unruly teenager by the hand and lead her to God's heavenly grace or to the ending that makes the author happy.

In your blessed and Holy names... AMEN.

Megan

A Reader's Un-Official Greeting to Other Fans

May I recommend the deMora starter pack? It's pretty much a necessity for any of her books, some more so than others.

1. Kleenex – Just buy a skid and save yourself the hassle of having to restock for each book. You won't necessarily need 'em for every book, but for the ones you do...damn. Just...yeah, one box probably won't cut it. (crying emoji)
2. Alcohol – I find that tequila or rum work equally well for drowning all the feels that her stories will give you. They tend to run the spectrum, from hysterical laugher, to bang-your-forehead-bloody frustration, to hucking-your-tablet-against-the-wall anger, to gaping-bloody-chestwound angst and hurt, to heart-bursting love. Her books will leave you raw and ragged in the best possible ways. Please ma'am, may I have another? (praying hands emoji, smile emoji, purple heart emoji)

3. BOB – Yeah, definitely a necessity, preferably of the rechargeable variety so you don't have to mess with having a truckload of batteries delivered. Alcohol ain't no good for drowning the feels that you'll need BOB for, all it does is make the fire burn hotter. (bonfire emoji)
4. Chocolate – Not a necessity for everyone, but definitely helps during the recovery process. (chocolate bar emoji)

Welcome to the group! (winkie emoji, big smile emoji)

Missy

THANK YOU!

ABOUT THE AUTHOR

Raised in the south, *Wall Street Journal* & *USA TODAY* bestselling author MariaLisa learned about the magic of books at an early age. Every summer, she would spend hours in the local library, devouring books of every genre. Self-described as a book-a-holic, she says "I've always loved to read, but then I discovered writing, and found I adored that, too. For reading...if nothing else is available, I've been known to read the back of the cereal box."

Want sneak peeks into what she's working on, or to chat with other readers about her books? Join the Facebook group! **bit.ly/deMora-FB-group**

deMora's got a spam-free newsletter list she'd love to have you join, too: **bit.ly/mldemora-newsletter**

~~~~~

My Rebel Wayfarers MC and the Neither This Nor That MC series do cross over, along with the Occupy Yourself band books, so readers have a couple of choices. The series can be read independently beginning with RWMC, OYBS, and then NTNT without too many spoilers. There's also a crossover between my RWMC world and Lila Rose's Hawks MC world. Or they can be read intertwined—in chronological order.

Here's the recommended reading order if you want to follow according to timing:

Mica, RWMC #1
A Sweet & Merry Christmas, RWMC #1.5
~~~~~

Slate, RWMC #2
Bear, RWMC #3
Born Into Trouble, OYBS #1
Jase, RWMC #4
Gunny, RWMC #5
Mason, RWMC #6
Hoss, RWMC #7
This Is the Route of Twisted Pain, NTNT #1
Harddrive Holidays, RWMC #7.5
Duck, RWMC #8
Biker Chick Campout, RWMC #8.5
Watcher, RWMC #9
Treading the Traitor's Path: Out Bad, NTNT #2
Living Without, Lila Rose's Hawks MC: Caroline Springs #4
Shelter My Heart, NTNT #3
A Kiss to Keep You, RWMC #9.25
Gun Totin' Annie, RWMC #9.5
Secret Santa, RWMC #9.75
Trapped by Fate on Reckless Roads, NTNT #4
Bones, RWMC #10
Gunny's Pups, RWMC #10.25
Not Even A Mouse, RWMC #10.75
Road Runner's Ride, RWMC #12.5
Never Settle, RWMC #10.5
Fury, RWMC #11
Christmas Doings, RWMC #11.25
Gypsy's Lady, RWMC #11.5
Thunderstruck, NTNT #5
Going Down Easy
No Man's Land
Cassie, RWMC #12

~~~~~
~~~~~

Also by MariaLisa deMora

Neither This Nor That MC romance series

Legends are born from moments like these. Folktales spun around a single point in time so perfect, you can almost hear the click resonating through the universe as things align. Meet Twisted, Po'Boy, Retro, and Ragman, good old boys from southern states who have many things in common. First, is a bone-deep love of the biker lifestyle. Second, would be their love of the brotherhood, and knowing that you trust the man at your back. Finally, these men have the love of a good woman. None of these come without a price, and it is our pleasure to journey along with them as they discover the blessings that can be won, and lost along the way.

This is the Route of Twisted Pain
Treading the Traitor's Path: Out Bad
Shelter My Heart
Trapped by Fate on Reckless Roads
Thunderstruck

5-Star Reviews for the stories of the NTNT MC series

This is the Route of Twisted Pain
"This is the Route of Twisted Pain is an exhilarating, gripping romance novel contrived of incredible world building, complex yet relatable characters, and a unique, captivating plot.

Gifted storyteller MariaLisa deMora beautifully balances exciting suspense, fast action, intriguing secrets with delicious, blazing hot romance scenes.
Readers will be up all night with this riveting page-turner."
~ NY Literary Magazine

I am completely tickled in my fancy for TWISTED!
First off, let me state that there was one thing I didn't like about this book and that is the LAST PAGE! I hated for it to end. I dearly loved this book and its characters as well as their setting.
~Colleen M.

Gripping tale
Twisted and Penny fit together beautifully. The book covers so much more than just their love story. Great introduction to the Incoherent MC. The tale is gripping and gritty. The journey is full of twists and turns that keep you on the edge of your seat. I couldn't put it down. Cannot wait for the next one.
~Lillmil

Twisted is one of the most original and interesting characters I have read in a long time. Marialisa's character building is setting a high bar for her to follow, she will hopefully continue with Po'Boy's story. The Route of Twisted Pain was pure brilliance, and I highly recommend this read.
~Penny T.

This book obsessed me!
This may be the best book I read all year.
These people...they're not characters, they're real... have stuck in my head from the day I met them.

MariaLisa deMora can throw words down that'll Twist (hehe) your insides up till you can't breathe for waiting to hear what's next!
I'm working my way through her other 'families' and yup....she really is that good.
~DeLane

Treading the Traitor's Path: Out Bad
"Treading the Traitor's Path: Out Bad is a solidly engrossing, well-written novel by a talented author.
MariaLisa deMora delivers a thrilling ride filled with exciting suspense, deliciously explicit, vivid sex scenes, and gritty, fast-paced action. Her characters are smart, complex, and strong with sharp edges. The settings meticulously detailed. Fans of Motorcycle Club romance stories will not want to miss this second installment in deMora's exciting series."
~ NY Literary Magazine
What an amazing read! DeMora does not simply wrote a book, she pulls you into a different world. When you read her work, you are very much surrounded by the characters and setting. Prepare for a book hangover because once you finish the book, you will still be stuck with Po Boy.
~KW

THIS WAS AMAZING. Highly recommend for a good story line, interesting characters. I just wish there was more more more.
~Laura

Loved This Book!
What did I just read?! Is my kindle still working? I'm pretty sure it combusted into flames while reading this story. RED HOT READ for 2017. Not what I was expecting at all! I tend to stay away from ménage a trois, because for me it's hard to

say there's any kind of conflict except for jealousy, and the ending kind of leaves things unresolved and unrealistic. NOT THIS BOOK! The best one out there guaranteed.
~Linda A

...seriously this series is just WTF so freaking good. Dark, Twisted, harsh, painful and raw. Po'Boy lives for his club, his brothers and his family, there is nothing he wouldn't do for them.
~Fay

I live and breathe for books like this! Fabulously Naughty!...Wickedly Hot! This is my first book by MariaLisa deMora and it will not be my last. MariaLisa delivered a 5 STAR READ! The plot is filled with action, suspense, romance and tons of hot scenes.
~Jenny F

~~~~~

Alace Sweets, a dark romantic suspense standalone

A dark thriller, this book is not a light read. Filled with edge-of-your-seat suspense, this intense story commands the reader's attention as it drives towards the explosive ending. Alace Sweets is a vigilante serial killer, with everything that implies and is sure to trip all your triggers. Be ready.

At seventeen, Alace Sweets turned a corner in her life, taking the wrong shortcut home from school.
~~~~~

Resisting the harsh knowledge her attackers will never be made to pay for their actions, Alace takes a stand. Justice must be served, and if fate's scales are out of balance, she's determined to set things right as best she can.

When the laws of men fail, the rules of Alace prevail.

5-Star Reviews for Alace Sweets

"Whatever deep dark trench [deMora] pulled a character like Alace from should be revisited again and often."
~Confessions of a Serial Reader

"deMora has a superb story-line and exceptional character development. All of her characters have such depth that will intrigue the reader..."
~Turning Another Page

"Hot, sweet, dark thriller."
~Beth D

"It will keep you on the edge of your seat and give you chills."
~Escape Reality Book Blog

"Disturbing, haunting, sickly; yet hot, sexy and heart racing!"
~Amanda L

"From the first page [deMora] pulls you into the world she has created and you do not even try to escape..."
~Little Shop of Readers Blog

“A must read for all those dark, gritty romance fans out there.”
~Sweet & Spicy Reads

“You will find yourself so drawn into the story that the outside world is blocked out and your locking the doors and turning on all the lights.”
~Danena F

“Don't judge me for bonding with a vigilante serial killer, she's more than what she does.”
~iScream Books

“Thrilling...chilling...full of suspense, nail biting edge of your seat excitement.”
~Tracey H

“Every time MariaLisa deMora picks up her pen (or opens her computer), she creates characters you want to believe in.”
~Gail S

“Intriguing dark storyline, beautiful love story and nail-biting conclusion, what more could a reader ask for?”
~Manda M

“This book takes you a dark and twisted ride that is gripping...”
~Renee Entress' Blog

“This book is dark and gritty and I literally had to take a day off from reading it because it's that intense.”
~My Girlfriend's Couch

"This is my favourite book so far from this author ... I recommend this book if you enjoy dark romantic thrillers."
~Cheekypee Reads and Reviews

"There's not enough stars to give this book and 5 just doesn't really do it justice!"
~DeLane C

"I couldn't put this book down from page one! Tried to stop & go to bed but couldn't sleep thinking about Alace and got up & finished the book."
~Debbie M

"MariaLisa DeMora, wordsmith that she is, made this a story of the enlightenment of a woman and finding love in a life where she has had none."
~Kat W

ADDITIONAL SERIES AND BOOKS

Please note that books in a series frequently feature characters from additional books within that series. If series books are read out of order, readers will twig to spoilers for the other books, so going back to read the skipped titles won't have the same angsty reveals.

Rebel Wayfarers MC series:

Mica, #1
A Sweet & Merry Christmas, #1.5
Slate, #2
Bear, #3
Jase, #4
Gunny, #5
Mason, #6
Hoss, #7
Harddrive Holidays, #7.5
Duck, #8
Biker Chick Campout, #8.5
Watcher, #9
A Kiss to Keep You, #9.25
Gun Totin' Annie, #9.5
Secret Santa, #9.75
Bones, #10
Gunny's Pups, #10.25
Never Settle, #10.5
Not Even A Mouse, #10.75
Fury, #11
Christmas Doings, #11.25
Gypsy's Lady, #11.5
Cassie, #12
Road Runner's Ride, #12.5

Occupy Yourself band series:

Born Into Trouble, #1
Grace In Motion, #2 (TBD)
What They Say, #3 (TBD)

Neither This, Nor That MC series:

This Is the Route Of Twisted Pain, #1
Treading the Traitor's Path: Out Bad, #2
Shelter My Heart, #3
Trapped by Fate on Reckless Roads, #4
Thunderstruck, #5

Rebel Wayfarers & Incoherent MC (NTNT) crossover stories:

Going Down Easy
No Man's Land

Mayhan Bucklers MC series:

Most Rikki-Tik, #1
Mad Minute, #2
Pucker Factor, #3
Boocoo Dinky Dau, #4

Borderline Freaks MC series:

Service and Sacrifice, #1
More Than Enough, #2
Lack of Inbetween, #3
See You in Valhalla, #4

If You Could Change One Thing:
Tangled Fates Stories

There Are Limits, #1
Rules Are Rules, #2
The Gray Zone, #3

Other Books:

With My Whole Heart
Bet On Us
Alace Sweets
Hard Focus
Dirty Bitches MC: Season 3

More information available at **mldemora.com**.

CPSIA information can be obtained
at www.ICGtesting.com
Printed in the USA
BVHW071932150919
558489BV00001B/120/P